BANDITS AND BALL GOWNS

BOOK 5 OF THE FAIRY TALES OF THE MAGICORUM

CHRISTINA BAUER

COPYRIGHT

Newton, MA 02464
www.monsterhousebooks.com
ISBN 9781946677617

DEDICATION

**For All Those Who Kick Ass, Take Names,
and Read Books**

CONTENTS

ALSO BY CHRISTINA BAUER

APPENDIX

AUTHOR'S NOTE

Dear Readers,

I wanted to give you a heads-up about a few changes to the style of this series. As an avid reader myself, I know that sticking with a certain series is a kind of sacred trust. If authors make huge changes mid-stream, it can throw off your enjoyment.

Here's a quick list of what I've altered and why. This way, you can make an informed decision if this book is for you.

Four Points of View

BANDITS AND BALL GOWNS includes chapters written from the point of view of both Alec and Elle, just like what happened in the last book, SLIPPERS AND THIEVES. However, this novel also includes chapters in the voices of two new characters, namely Jacoby and Agatha. It's a lot of folks to juggle and I've tried to group stuff together in order to keep things moving. Hopefully, it works!

Three Books

This novel is book two in the Cinderella part of my Magicorum series. To give all the storylines enough time, I've decided to break it up into three books. First was SLIPPERS AND THIEVES, second is BANDITS AND BALLGOWNS, and the third (and probably final) Cinderella story will be FIRE AND CINDER, which will be released in the spring of 2021.

Here's what happened. As I got into the story of Elle and Agatha, I really felt like their inner journeys needed more focus and closure. As a result, this book is more about internal battles versus big magical fights.

One Cliff

Normally, I end my books on a happily ever after. This one ends on a cliff and there is some hanging. Sorry, it's what this story wanted to be.

More Than Ten Images

On a final note, I love trying new things and wanted to see if there's a middle place between graphic novels and text-only books, especially for a story like BANDITS AND BALL GOWNS.

Growing up, my favorite book was a moth-eaten version of the original GRIMM'S FAIRY TALES. I loved the dark storytelling in this compilation, but I positively adored the imagery.

With BANDITS AND BALL GOWNS, I wanted to expand on the Grimms' original visual approach by adding in lots of fantasy art. I already describe things a ton, but since a picture is worth a thousand words, I thought this might make my world building more immersive for readers like you.

As a result, there are more than ten images in this novel. Virtually all of the pictures were created by artists who specialize in 3D computer rendering. If you like this approach, please let me know! It's a lot of extra work, but I do feel it enhances the experience.

Conclusion

Well, that's it from me in terms of a heads-up about

the new text-n-graphics extravaganza on the pages ahead.

Fingers crossed that you'll enjoy it!

- *Christina Bauer, author*

BANDITS AND BALL GOWNS

ELLE

MANHATTAN

"*E*lle, Elle, we want Elle!"

Loud voices wrench me out of deep sleep. Jamming my pillow over my head, I try muffling the noise. *No go.* More ear-splitting yells come through, loud and clear.

"Elle, Elle, we want Elle!"

What a coincidence. I want to punch you all in the throat for waking me up.

No question who's breaking my personal sound barrier. Enchanted humans are marching outside my apartment building. *Again.* All while screaming my name. *Again.*

"Come out, Elle! We want you!"

It isn't clear what they'd *do* with me if they ever *got* me. I can't imagine it's anything good.

None of this is a surprise, by the way. For weeks, these supernatural stalkers have been drawn to me like subway rats to a dropped Egg McMuffin. It's because I'm Magicorum, meaning I'm one of the lucky folks whose future is locked into a *fairy tale life template*. In my case, that's Cinderella.

The chanting starts up once more. "Elle, Elle, we want our Cindereeeeeeeeella!"

Sadly, whatever's happening here is related to the dark side of my fairy tale life template. Being Cinderella isn't just ball gowns and glass slippers. There's a reason it's called the *Grimm's Fairy Tales*, not the *Chipper Funtime Stories*. When magic gets into the mix, stuff turns ugly. Humans become enchanted. Shouting is involved. I eventually lose a shoe. You get the idea.

Not that I worry about it too much. I take my Cinderella-ness, kick it in the ass and call it a bitch. *Boom.*

Case in point. You may wonder how someone like me—meaning an eighteen-year old with a crappy life template—can afford my own apartment in Manhattan. Short answer: To make ends meet, I un-steal jewelry and run the occasional con. Don't judge. Fairy tale life templates are the pits.

"Elle! Get out here Eeeeeeeeeeeelle!"

Wow, they're really yappy this morning. That gets me curious. Rolling over, I peep through my window and scan the sidewalk below. Since my apartment is twenty stories up, I have the perfect view. Today, about thirty humans mill around the concrete. In most ways, they're typical New Yorkers. I count adults of all ages, sizes and nationalities. What makes this group unique is how their eyes all glow with a magical orange light. It's a look that says, *guess what? I'm totally possessed.* At least, that's how it appears to *moi.* Other humans can't detect anything strange about my stalkers. They're unable to even hear the chanting fiesta.

Suddenly, azure light flares beneath my bedroom door. A heavy charge fills the air, along with the faintest hint of ozone. *That would be a spell.* And based on the particular shade of sparkly blue which peeps across my carpet? Someone just magically transported themselves into the hallway outside my bedroom.

Unlike the stalkers, this is a good thing. Being Magicorum means more than getting dragged into a fairy tale future. We also wield the power of either witches, fae or shifters. In my case, I'm a fairy. And with my knowledge of the supernatural, I know exactly who just transported into my hallway: Alec Le Charme, expert warlock, prince of a jewelry empire, and (as of six weeks ago) my boyfriend. Cue angelic choir.

Gentle knocks sound. "Elle? It's Alec." His voice has the low rasp of a sleepy guy. So cute. "Time to study your enchanted humans again."

Joy bubbles up inside me. "Come on in."

The door swings open. Today, Alec's the definition of charming with his sleepy eyes, muscular frame, low hanging jeans and white T-shirt. Alec is also barefoot, which absolutely kills me. I'm such a sucker for *hot guy feet*.

Alec pauses on the threshold. "What's today's variety?" No question what he means here. Alec is obsessed with my PJ collection.

I gesture across my torso. "Dancing yetis."

He shakes his head. "Where do you find these?"

I bob my brows. "I have my ways."

The world seems to collapse until it's just me and Alec. An electric sense of awareness pulses between us. Since Alec is my first kiss, he insists that we take things slowly in the romance department. That said, if Alec gets anywhere near me right now, I'm tackling him, linebacker-style.

Alec shoots me a sly grin. He absolutely knows what I'm thinking. "Are you open for dinner this evening, by any chance?"

"Let me check." I look around the room as if my schedule's written on the walls. "Why, yes. I happen to be available. My roomie is off on an adventure."

"What a coincidence," says Alec. "My roommate is away as well." Alec lives with Knox, who's dating my own roomie, Bry. Both are gone on a secret quest that's led by none other than the Magicorum's most famous dragon shifter, a fae named Colonel Mallory the Magnificent. Also joining them is a mysterious fairy, the Queen of Hearts.

And did I mention that their mission is a total mystery? *It is.* I don't even know when Bry and company will return. Major bummer.

Across the room, Alec plunks onto his favorite chair. "I brought my notebook." To accent this point, Alec waves the leather volume I gave him weeks ago. The cover reads, *Operation Bag The Baddie.*

Here's what we've figured out so far. Someone's enchanting humans to march underneath my window. Since I'm a Cinderella life template, the driving force behind this ugliness *should* be my evil stepfamily. But Marchesa, Ivy and Agatha are all in exile. That's why Alec and I are on the hunt for the real culprits. By tracking *what* happens and *when* with my stalkers, we figure a clue is bound to show up eventually.

Alec holds up his pen. "Let's start with messages.

How many signs are the humans holding? What do the words actually say?"

Leaning my forehead against the glass pane, I make some quick calculations. "Thirty-three humans are traipsing around down there. Sixteen carry signs. All say the same thing. *Pick a new prince, Elle!*"

Six weeks ago, Alec and I started dating at the world-famous Glass Slipper Ball. For some reason, my human stalkers want me to find a new boyfriend.

Meh. They can stick it.

Alec scribbles on the sheet before him. "That makes two-hundred and forty-seven times that sign has appeared in the last six weeks. It's your most popular message."

"Whoever's casting this spell, they want you gone."

"I'd like to see them try and get rid of me." Alec's eyes light up with fire and determination. Waves of power and magic roll off him, filling the room with his presence.

Tackling is definitely becoming an attractive option again.

Stay focused, Elle.

I look down at the sidewalk once more. A different face appears in the mix of enchanted humans. This new woman stands out for two reasons. First, she's dressed up as a sheriff from the Old West. That doesn't happen often, even in New York. Second, her eyes are regular blue instead of glowing orange.

In my personal stalker history, that's never happened before. Enchanted humans are their own bubble of strangeness. No one without orange eyes gets anywhere near them. Yet this sheriff stands right in the middle of the pack.

Could it be a clue?

I scooch closer to the windowpane and try for a better look. But when I check again, the mysterious woman is gone.

Alec snaps his notebook shut. "Sadly, I have to run."

"More Le Charme fun?"

Alec rolls his eyes. "Welcome to my new life of suck."

Here's what that means. My family isn't the only one in exile. Alec's parents, Diamond and Legend, also got chucked off into the Faerie Lands. *Good riddance.* Since then, Alec has become the new CEO of Le Charme. It's as much fun as it sounds.

"Good luck with that," I state. "Go meet the people. Sign the things. Crush the lesser jewelry guys. Woot."

"And so I shall. But not until I'm certain you've safely arrived at West Lake Prep. These enchanted humans worry me." Alec offers me his hand. "May I transport you to school, Milady?"

What a man. Alec runs a multinational company

while finishing off his high school degree online. In other words, he's a super-busy guy. That's why it means the world to me how—even with so much happening— Alec still wants to transport my butt around.

With that realization, warmth and love radiate through my soul. My affection swells so high, I totally give up on my *not-tackling plan*. Crossing the room, I wrap my arms around Alec's neck. His skin feels warm and smooth under my touch. As our bodies press together, excitement swirls within me. Going on tiptoe, I press my mouth to Alec's. His lips are soft and firm; our connection sends a slow burn through my core.

I smile into our kiss. "I'll take you up on that transport spell."

"Can you be ready in twenty?"

"You know it."

"Good."

Alec steps away, reaches into his pocket and pulls out a huge sapphire. Magical gems are how wizards like Alec enact their spells. Using that stone, my boyfriend will transport back to his own apartment. Alec lifts his fist. As he begins his spell, blue light shines between his fingers. Tiny points of sapphire-colored brightness rise from his hand and then multiply. Soon it looks as if Alec is surrounded by a column of miniature shooting stars.

Alec's pillar of brightness flares with more power. A moment later, Alec is gone.

But I know he'll return. Alec gave his word.

ALEC

MANHATTAN

7:29 AM
I just dropped off Elle at school. Now I stand in the board room of the famous Le Charme building in Midtown Manhattan.

As the CEO.

I certainly look the role, especially with my new buzz cut. *Serious times call for serious hair* and all that. Still, the new job doesn't seem real. How did I ever end up running the world's largest jewelry chain at eighteen years old?

Oh, that's right.

My parents magically tortured me. In punishment, they got chucked into exile. Now I'm running my family's company.

Long story short, this is not your typical fairy tale.

Around me, the board room is a mixture of new and old. One entire wall is formed from windows that show off a view of the Manhattan skyline.

That's the new part.

But the rest of the chamber looks like something from an old vampire castle. A long wooden table dominates the space. Dark Persian rugs cover the floor. Paintings of unhappy-looking old dudes stare down from the walls. It's enough to make my skin crawl.

It's also why I stand at the head of the table and close to the exit. That way, I can speed for the door if I get really creeped out.

One old white guy sits nearby. It's the Chairman of the Board of Le Charme Jewelers, a fellow by the name of Duchismo El Grande. He's the most wrinkly guy in the company, which might be why everyone calls him the Duke.

I glance at the clock. 7:30 AM

"It is time," says the Duke. He always announces when meetings begin and I let him. To be honest, I'm not sure if the guy has another purpose in life.

"Thank you, Duke."

After I slip off my suit coat, I set the garment onto the back of my chair. This'll be a long day; it's best to get comfortable.

"Would you like to sit down?" asks the Duke.

"I'll stand. What do you need?"

"I want to discuss next week's annual board meeting. This will be your first one. Let's ensure you're prepared for the day. Some of the practices at Le Charme Jewelers are unconventional."

"Really? Like what?"

"To begin with, your parents always start off annual board meetings by leading everyone in a group sing of *So This Is Love.*"

I do a double-take. "You've got to be kidding."

The Duke lifts his chin. "No."

"Let me get this straight. You want everyone to sing, *So This is Love*, as in a song from the cartoon Cinderella?"

"It's an animated film, not a cartoon," corrects the Duke. "And the answer is *yes*. Obviously, it would be that song."

"Official decree number 347." By the way, I'm a boss at this aspect of CEO life. *Official decrees are my thing.* "We'll no longer start annual board meetings with music."

The Duke pales. "But we have musicians who come in and perform while we sing along. They are expecting to attend the meeting."

I raise my hand. "Official decree number 348. No more second-guessing my official decrees."

There, that told him.

The Duke clears his throat. "If you insist."

"I do. Don't you need a pen or something? I can't help but notice how you aren't writing any of this down."

"I shall never forget that you refuse to sing our corporate song, my Prince."

"My name is Alec." So far, I've done six official decrees for folks to stop calling me their prince. Hasn't stuck so far.

"I shall endeavor to remember that, my Prin—"

"Alec."

The Duke clears his throat. "Yes, Prince Alec. At the board meeting, we'll also need you to review various contracts and papers." The Duke fidgets with a stack of documents before him. I can't help but notice the names atop one sheet.

Marchesa, Ivy and Agatha Cynder.

I swipe the document from the stack. "This looks interesting."

"No, Prince Alec!" The Duke makes grabby hands to get the sheet back, but he's not too nimble these days.

I scan the text. "This is a report from someone named L. Cloake. It appears she's been tracking the movements of the Cynder family while they're exiled in the Faerie lands." I give more of the document a quick look. "They've been crisscrossing different fiefdoms, looking for support." I round on the Duke. "Why wasn't I told about this?"

The Duke frowns. "I've never seen that thing before. Who is the Cynder family?"

"Please. I'm dating a member of the Cynder family. Her name is Elle, remember?"

"I'm a very old man. Your personal romances are of no concern to me."

"Elle's mother and stepsisters were sent off into exile with my parents. Don't pretend you aren't aware."

The Duke hangs his head. "This is all very confusing."

Sure, it is. The Duke plays at being the doddering old guy, but he's sharp as a dagger when it suits him.

I fold up the sheet and set it into my pocket. "This meeting is over."

The Duke extends his wrinkly arm. "Aren't you going to give that back?"

"No, I'm marching right over to security since the report says they're the ones who authorized this surveillance. I want to find out who's hiring spies to follow my girlfriend's family around and then failing to tell me about it."

The Duke taps the loose skin of his cheek. "Come to think of it, I might remember something about that contract."

"Your chance to tell the truth is over." Leaning forward, I rest my hands on the table. "I need your honesty, Duke. Without it, there's no place for you here."

"I understand, my Pr—" The Duke clears his throat. "I mean, my Prince Alec."

"I suppose that's good enough for now." Patting the sheet in my pocket, I head out the door and make a beeline for the elevator bank.

Time to have a conversation with the Head of Security.

Because I'll do anything to protect my Elle.

3

ELLE

*T*ransporting to school with Alec was a total treat. We materialized right in the main reception hall of West Lake Prep.

By the way, that wasn't an easy thing to do. Once you're at school, you can leave easily enough. But entering? Not so simple. West Lake Prep has been warded to the hilt in order to keep magic users out. So the fact that Alec popped right in?

Mega warlock stuff.

The first few times Alec brought me to West Lake, he'd stare wistfully around the halls. Clearly, my boyfriend wanted to be back at school. Lately, he's been too busy to care. Today we shared a quick kiss and then Alec went off to his CEO gig.

Which brings me to the present moment. I sit in the

back row of *Fae Spells for Dummies* class. Forty students —both boys and girls—sit in desks that are aligned into neat rows. The chairs here are specially designed so wings can fit through.

Every color in the spectrum is arrayed out before me. There are silver wings and gold ones. Bright and dark. Shimmery and matte. Patterns, solid colors and something in-between. The teacher, Miss Morningdew, goes on about the best ways to use fairy dust in spells. Meanwhile, everyone's wings slowly beat in a unified rhythm. The many colors shift and sparkle with gentle movements.

It's enough to make my heart crack with sorrow.

As a child, my fairy wings were removed to keep me safely hidden from anyone who might want to steal my magic. Today my wings may be gone, but my fae side hasn't forgotten them. The need to fly is a constant ache inside my soul.

Here's the semi-scary thing. Although I attend West Lake Prep to be near Bry and Knox, a twisted part of me likes hanging in the fae section of school. That way, I can check out other people's wings. It's as healthy as it sounds.

Don't stare, Elle. You'll just get depressed.

As it happens, there's a big bank of windows to my left that overlook the school's private park. This is New

York, so it's more of a postage stamp than a major recreational area. Still, it's better than staring at things I no longer have. Angling my head, I force myself to check out the greenery.

Hey, there are some bushes.

Wow. Trees, too.

What do you know? A bench.

And I'm out of sightseeing ideas.

I return to watching everyone's wings once more. It's as mopey as it gets. Along my back, long-atrophied muscles try to flex wings that are no longer there. The demand is enough to make my shoulders ache.

In front of the class, Miss Morningdew pauses. She's a green fairy in a glimmering gown and matching egg-style hat. It should make her look like a matchstick, but it doesn't. That's the thing about being fae—you can wear anything and make it work.

"Today we'll explore something new," announces Miss Morningdew.

Everyone perks up. We spent four weeks learning how to use fairy dust to boil water. This is a big deal.

"Today we'll learn about the dark side of magic," continues Miss Morningdew.

All the fairies in class let out a low, "Oooooh, ahhhh."

I don't know how they do it, but fairies talk in unison all the time. I never participate, though.

Miss Morningdew waves her arm. A two-dimensional picture appears in the air: a blue man with a bare torso. Where his legs should be, there's only a coil of smoke.

"This is…" Miss Morningdew takes in a long breath. "A genie."

Miss Morningdew is a big fan of dramatic pauses. I've learned to tune them out over time.

"As we all know," continues Miss Morningdew, "genies are the crackpots of the Magicorum world. They all start off as regular shifters, witches or fae with a single fairy tale life template. But then… they change." Miss Morningdew rounds on me. "Elle, please stand up."

I tap my chest. "Me?"

"Yes, this is necessary for the class."

Little by little, I rise.

"Who can tell me what's different about Elle?"

"She doesn't have any wings," recites everyone in unison.

"Correct," says Miss Morningdew. "As I said, all genies start off as regular Magicorum. Then one thing changes, like how Elle has no wings."

I stifle the urge to roll my eyes. Fairies are mean creatures, by and large. But then it comes to being nasty, Miss Morningdew is a true artist.

"Who can tell me what happens next?" asks Miss Morningdew.

"She'll dissolve," replies the class.

"Exactly," declares Miss Morningdew. "When Magicorum dissolve, that means they slide into a new fairy tale life template. For instance, Elle might start off as a Cinderella but then become attracted to a new template, such as one that supports being a thief. In other words, Elle could dissolve from Cinderella to Aladdin. Once that happens, it wouldn't be long before Elle becomes a genie."

My stomach sinks. *Does Miss Morningdew know that I un-steal jewelry on the side?*

For the record, when I say *un-steal jewelry*, I mean that I find lost stuff and claim the reward. Still, the process involves some breaking and entering, not to mention a bunch of untruths. So I keep it on the down low.

"What do you think, Elle?" asks Miss Morningdew. "Would you ever steal?"

Fae can't lie, as a rule. Fortunately, it's one of my strong suits. I set my hand over my heart. "Never."

"Oh, my," declares Miss Morningdew. "The way I understand it, you both lie and steal. That's a lot like an Aladdin fairy tale template. Would you ever want to become a genie?"

"I'm happy as a Cinderella, thank you very much."

"That's good," says Miss Morningdew. "After all, there are so few genies left these days. If you became one, you'd spend all eternity roaming the world without any friends. And your mind would snap. You'd become... insane."

All of a sudden, I notice how the blue genie image has changed. It's no longer a bolshy blue guy with no shirt and wispy legs. Nope.

Now it's a girl my age who's dressed as a sheriff. As in, this is the exact same girl I saw this morning on my sidewalk.

To make matters worse, the girl turns right to me, crosses her eyes and sticks out her tongue. That's classic genie behavior, right there. She then points to her face and mouths a name. *Skye.*

Oh, oh. This can't be good.

4

ELLE

For a long second, I can only stare at the floating image of an Old West chick whispering the name Skye, over and over.

I've seen a lot of weird stuff, but even for me, this is new territory.

Then again, maybe it's part of today's lesson. I point to the image of Skye. "Who is that, Miss Morningdew?"

Turning, the teacher focuses on the floating picture once more. Only now, it's back to being a blue guy with mist for legs.

"It's just a generic blue genie," Miss Morningdew replies. "He doesn't have a name." She stalks closer. "Are you feeling all right, Elle? Did all this talk about your missing wings… upset you?"

At this point, everyone in class is watching the

Torture Elle Show. Again, this is typical stuff for fae. Our people pair gorgeous faces with sadistic personalities. This is why I hang out in the back of the room and just watch wings most of the time.

"As a matter of fact, all this wing-talk did upset me," I explain. "I'd like to go home early and cry now."

Which is only partly true. Still, I know how my people work. If Miss Morningdew thinks I'm heading home in order to play video games, then she'll never let me leave. But if I'm taking off to suffer? That's all fine and dandy.

Sure enough, I'm totally right.

In short order, I'm back in the main reception hall at school. Everyone's in class now, so the place is deserted. I check my locker to get my stuff, and that's when I realize my big miss.

I left my plus-ten Cloak Of Hiding at home.

By wearing that garment, I can walk the streets without being mobbed by stalkers. Without it, I need another way home. I try texting Alec. Sadly, the Le Charme building gets spotty reception at best. My messages don't go through.

That's when it hits me. I'm already really good at using my fairy magic to boil water. Maybe it's time to try casting a transport spell of my own. It's got to be easier than either walking through stalkers or asking other fae at school for help.

I nod once, the decision made. I'm casting a spell and transporting my butt.

Closing my eyes, I summon my inner magic. A whirlwind of pink sparkles surrounds me. *The spell has begun.* I picture my living room.

The pink haze grows thicker until I can no longer make out the details of the school around me. Then the colored mist gets lighter. Soon a hazy view of my living room appears. The scene solidifies. I'm home again and smiling.

The spell worked.

Only, it feels really cold in here. I'm about to check our thermostat when I notice the truth.

I'm naked.

A rustling sounds behind me. Every nerve in my body goes on alert. Little by little, I turn around.

Alec is here. Oh, hell.

Now Alec and I have kissed and such. But I've certainly never been naked in front of him before. So I do what any normal person would under these circumstances.

I lunge across the room and hide behind the couch.

"Elle? Are you all right?" I'd wonder why Alec sounds

so calm and smooth, but then again, he's wearing clothes.

Seconds tick by.

How long have I been hiding behind large furniture and panicking? Too long probably. I take in a deep breath, preparing myself to sound suave and confident. Or, as much as you can while hiding naked behind your couch.

"I'm fine." Sadly, the words come out about two octaves higher than normal. I try again. "Can you get me something to wear?"

"Sure." I hear footsteps as Alec walks into my bedroom, followed by the rustle of drawers opening and closing.

And that's when I realize my big mistake.

I just told Alec to rifle through my underwear drawer. *Ugh.* This just keeps getting worse and worse.

A minute later, some clothes land beside me on the living room floor. It's my fancy underwear set along with a black cocktail dress. Oh, and heels. It seems Alec wants to complete the look.

I peer over the couch. "You brought out a cocktail dress?"

Alec winks. "You know how I love you in a formal look."

I shoot him the side-eye. "Okay, Mister Fancypants. Close your eyes and I'll get something *real* to wear."

"A cocktail dress is real."

Using my pointer and middle fingers, I gesture right at his eyes. "Close them."

Alec let out a long-suffering sigh. "If you insist."

With Alec no longer watching, I pad into my bedroom and shut the door. A few minutes later, I step out in a pair of black jeans along with a T-shirt celebrating the best 80's hair band ever, Cinderella. Alec is now sitting on the couch while gripping a sheet of paper so tightly, his knuckles are white.

I sit down beside him. "What's wrong?"

"This." Alec hands over the sheet.

What I see is a shocker.

"Let me get this straight," I begin. "According to this report, someone named L. Cloake has been following my stepfamily around the Faerie Lands. Apparently, Marchesa, Ivy and Agatha have been meandering about and looking for someone to help them escape. Not that I'd expect anything less... but how did you get this?"

"The Duke had it."

"What? As in the Chairman of the Board at Le Charme?"

"One and the same. The sheet says the report was commissioned by the security team at Le Charme, but they know nothing about it. I cast my highest-level truth spells on them. Twice."

"What about the Duke?"

"My parents warded him against unwanted spells years ago. The idea is to keep him safe from being brainwashed or whatever."

I lean back onto the couch and think this through. "If someone at Le Charme is watching my family, then you know they have tabs on Diamond and Legend as well."

"Agreed." Alec rubs his neck in a slow rhythm. "I don't like this. I've cast dozens of diving spells. I can't shake the feeling something is wrong, but I can't discover what it is."

"Fortunately for us, I know the perfect thing to do."

"What's that?"

"Play video games, order pizza and then kiss each other's faces off."

Alec's face lights up into a thousand-watt smile. "I love this concept."

I return his grin with one of my own. And as I fire up my gaming console, my thoughts return to how my stepfamily is now roaming around the Faerie Lands. I've no doubt that Marchesa and Ivy are perfectly fine and well-fed. Those two are tough as nails.

But Agatha is a kind soul. She's the type who'll give away her last meal before fighting for seconds. In fact, I never understood why she insisted on joining Ivy and Marchesa in exile anyway. I wouldn't be surprised if Agatha had zero to do with any of their evil plans.

So why would Agatha follow them to the Faerie Lands?

An odd sense of foreboding settles into my soul. I certainly hope Agatha is all right...

5

AGATHA

THE FAERIE LANDS

*S*huffle... *shuffle... shuffle...*

With slow steps, I trudge along the forest path. It takes all my focus, but I carefully arrange myself into the definition of one word.

Misery.

For me, acting gloomy is a key life skill. It allows me to hide in plain sight, all while limiting how much I interact with my family. On reflex, I think through my *sad girl checklist*.

Weepy eyes? Got 'em. I'm also working a single tear on my right cheek. That's what you call *an advanced mope skill.*

Mourning veil? I wear this thing like a pro.

Slumped shoulders? I've spent years honing how to curl myself forward just the right way.

All the while, I push up my inner sense of gloom. That really helps to nail the overall look. Normally, feeling morose comes pretty easily to me.

Not today.

Why? For years, I've dreamed of visiting one place. Now, I'm finally here.

The Faerie Lands. At last.

I can't help but soak in the landscape. Stout trees tower nearby, their hefty trunks topped by leafy branches. Blades of grass look so bright, they could be shards of emeralds. A clear blue sky arches overhead. Three yellow suns beam down. Butterflies flit everywhere. Pure happiness bubbles through me. It's tempting to grin my face off.

Keep frowning, Agatha. You know what happens when you lose the sad girl look.

Shifting my gaze, I see that reason right ahead of me: Ivy and Marchesa. If you asked Elle Cynder, she'd say Marchesa is my mother while Ivy's my sister. Together, the three of us make up the evil stepfamily for a Cinderella life template.

But it's all a lie.

Not sure how it goes for *other* evil stepsisters, but

this template doesn't work for me. I'm neither evil nor a stepsister.

As a matter of fact, I'm not even human.

I'm an elf. *A changeling.* Sadly, Marchesa's second baby died shortly after birth. I was swapped in by parties unknown. Around age eight, a silver mark appeared on my hip that shows a moon and three stars. This became my first clue to my non-human state. Soon afterward, I caught sight of my elf ears. They only appeared for a second. Even so, it was enough to get the general idea.

I don't belong.

Ever since then, I've been trying to discover my true identity. No luck yet.

But perhaps soon, I'll know everything.

Somewhere in the Faerie Lands, there's the Moonbeam Mirror, a magical object that shows the true nature of whoever looks into it. If I can find that thing, I'll know who I am at last. Just contemplating that mirror sends a warm sense of satisfaction through me.

Big mistake.

For hours, Ivy's stride has been smooth. Now she shivers.

Oh, no. It's happening again.

Somehow, that girl always knows when I get in a good mood. Ivy glances at me over her shoulder. In the soft light of the triple suns, Ivy is tall, bright-eyed, and graceful. She's so lovely, you'd think *she* was the elf in the family. Marchesa carries the same wide-eyed beauty. As the saying goes, it's only skin deep.

"What's your problem?" Ivy asks.

"Oh." I sigh. "Everything."

Ivy stops. "Liar. You're mighty pleased about something. And you have no right. We're in exile. For weeks, Mother and I have meandered forest paths in search of help."

And this, right here. This spontaneous lecture on how I suck is why I always work my inner sad girl. Interacting with Ivy or Marchesa is never pleasant. That said, when nasty words are sent my way, I don't exactly ignore them, either.

"I was meandering with you, right?" I ask. "You make it sound like you and Marchesa were alone."

"Don't be rude," counters Ivy.

"You're accusing me of being happy and now I'm being rude. Which is it?"

Ivy turns to Marchesa. "Mother, I need you. Aggie's being impossible."

"Agatha," I correct. I've been trying to stop the Aggie nickname since I was six years old.

Marchesa saunters over to pat Ivy's shoulder. "What's *the girl* doing now?"

In front of outsiders, I'm her cherished daughter Agatha. When it's just us three, I'm always *the girl*.

Ivy sniffles. "Aggie doesn't take our exile seriously."

"Again?" Marchesa rounds on me. "Why do you keep upsetting your sister, after all I've done for you? These past weeks, it's taken everything in me to keep us all fed and clothed."

"Don't I usually forage and cook?" I ask. "Or did I miss something?"

"You're so ungrateful." Ivy focuses on Marchesa. "She's about to wander away once more, mark my words."

I could shut up now, but I don't. Life gives me few pleasures. Talking back to Ivy and Marchesa is one of them.

"*I'm* wandering away?" I ask. "You two have been sneaking off on me, not the other way around."

As a matter of fact, I don't know where Ivy and Marchesa go, but I'm sure it's related to our destination for today's stroll. Which raises a question.

"Where are we headed, anyway?" I ask.

Ever since we three were exiled from Earth, Marchesa's been scheming to wreak her revenge on Elle and Alec. My guess is that she's found a willing ally... and *that's* whoever we're seeing today.

Ivy and Marchesa exchange a long look. A whole

conversation hides inside that stare. Eventually, Marchesa shrugs. "I suppose you'll find out soon enough. We've been summoned to the palace of Nal'Adel, the Mistress of Moonshadow."

My heart races. I have a moon-shaped birthmark on my hip, and Nal'Adel is the Mistress of Moonshadow. *Could I be part of Nal'Adel's court?*

The moment the thought arises, I press it away. Thinking about Nal'Adel will just send more joyful thoughts in my direction. That's the last thing I need right now.

I refocus on today's mission. "Let me guess. You've been sneaking off to visit Nal'Adel's court for awhile. But you've never brought me along before. Why am I joining you now?"

Ivy and Marchesa don't reply. Instead, the pair resume marching along the trail. Before, we all walked in silence. Now Ivy and Marchesa whisper together while occasionally glancing in my direction. I can't tell much of what they're saying, but the words *brat* and *impudent* come up a lot.

A thin white line cuts across the path ahead. The mark glows with ethereal light, so it's not something that humans like Ivy or Marchesa can see. But I pick it out easily enough.

It's a boundary.

That glowing line means we're about to pass from one fiefdom into another. In the Faerie Lands, that can be a dangerous thing to do. Right now, we're in the realm of sunshine. But beyond that border, who knows what we'll encounter?

I cup my hand by my mouth. "Be careful!"

If Ivy and Marchesa hear me, they don't show it. Instead, the pair march right across the line and vanish from view.

I follow.

Once I cross the boundary, the landscape instantly changes. A moment ago, everything was bathed in sunshine. Now, the world sits in shadow and mist. A giant moon hangs in the sky, its surface covered in semi-darkness. We all stand near the edge of a cliff, or so I assume. There's a rope bridge through the clouds to another outcropping of land.

The truth hits me with a wallop. No wonder Ivy and Marchesa didn't stop. They've been here before. This must be the realm of Nal'Adel.

A chill of awe prickles over my skin. What I know about the Faerie Lands, I learned from surfing Magic Web back in New York. That's how I learned about the Moonbeam Mirror. But there was never anything on magic Web about places like this one. It's both upsetting and beautiful, all at once.

"We're here." Marchesa then fluffs Ivy's hair. "You look lovely. Perfect for meeting the Mistress of Moonshadow."

Ivy grins. "Thank you." Turning, Ivy looks me over from head to toe and frowns. It's the kind of grimace she usually reserves for two occasions, namely particularly nasty roadkill or any assessment of my appearance.

Ivy sighs. "I wish you hadn't lost your hat."

"I didn't lose it," I correct. "Some pixies stole it."

On reflex, I pull my veil more tightly around my head. Every once in a while, I get strong emotions and unconsciously cast a spell. Sometimes it's cool stuff, like when I helped Elle escape from Marchesa. Other times, my elven ears just show up out of nowhere. But I never know when that'll happen, so I always keep some headgear on.

"I wish we could hide her face," states Marchesa. "Losing that floppy hat is a catastrophe."

Once more, here's where I should keep my mouth shut. But I don't.

"That's a little extreme," I counter. "I lost a hat, not a nuclear missile."

Marchesa shoots me the side-eye. "Without your hat, all these beautiful fae will see how your makeup runs down your face. It's like having a clown in the family."

Ivy tries to hide her giggle behind her hand. She

doesn't work too hard at it, though. "What a mess you are."

This is one of the odd facts about being me, by the way. I don't even wear mascara and yet it still runs down my face. Chalk it up to a strange side effect of being magical.

The mists rise and congeal into the form of a gaunt woman in gray body armor. Her pale skin is highlighted by dark, inset eyes while her hair is piled atop her head in a messy bun. But that's not the strangest part of her appearance. This lady's mouth is covered over by a single sheet of skin. I remember the lyrics from a human song.

> Oh, I'm bein' followed by a moonshadow,
> moonshadow, moonshadow...
> And if I ever lose my mouth,
> all my teeth, north and south
> Yes if I ever lose my mouth,
> Oh if I won't have to talk...

This woman certainly lost her mouth, but can she still speak?

As if in reply, the woman lifts a claw-tipped hand up to her jaw and tears off the skin covering her lips. The flesh tears away like it's already dead, revealing an overly wide mouth and pointed teeth.

"I'm Lady Cloake," she says in a deep and rasping voice.

I gasp. She's scary as hell. And for the first time, I realize the true risk here.

Marchesa and Ivy want to ruin Elle and Alec. Yet by creating an alliance with Nal'Adel, they could end up destroying us all.

LADY CLOAKE

6

AGATHA

Ivy and Marchesa curtsey. "Greetings, Lady Cloake," they say in unison.

I shake my head. And just a few minutes ago, I was the one trying to warn them that we were heading into another fiefdom. Meanwhile, it might have been helpful for them to share how Nal'Adel has a terrifying guard.

Lady Cloake raises her arms. Lines of black shadow curl up from the misty ground, their shapes reminding me of wide ribbons. The strips rise to surround all four of us like the bars in a cage.

We're closed in.

This time, I know to look at Ivy and Marchesa for clues as to what's going on. Neither of them seem worried, so I'm guessing this is just how things work with Lady Cloake.

So far, so good.

Lady Cloake snaps her fingers; more dark ribbons of shadow rise up. These wrap around me, mummy-style, holding me in place. Alarm rattles down my spine. I shoot another glance at my so-called family. Ivy looks shocked but happy. Marchesa seems wary.

I'm guessing this *isn't* something that happens.

Lady Cloake steps up to me and eyes me carefully. My heart pounds so hard, I'll be surprised if I don't crack a rib. Reaching forward, Lady Cloake grabs my chin. Her cold claws dig into my warm flesh.

On reflex, I try to twist away from her grasp. The shadow bindings hold me perfectly in place.

Little by little, Lady Cloake leans in closer. When her mouth is by my neck, she inhales deeply.

Looking into my soul, I try to see if I can access any of my inner magic. Not that I know how to wield it. Still, if Lady Cloake is going to attack, it could be my only defense.

But my magic stays firmly out of reach.

Long moments pass. At last, Lady Cloake steps backward. She snaps her fingers; my shadow bindings fall away.

"You may go," she tells me.

Ivy steps forward. "Wait a second. I thought Nal'Adel wanted to assess her?"

"And that's what I just did," replies Lady Cloake in her deep voice. "She's a worthless human."

"Aren't you going to kill her?" asks Ivy. "I heard Nal'Adel has a special altar for that."

"Hey, now," I declare. "No one said anything about killing."

Technically, no one said anything to me at all. But with any luck, Lady Cloake thinks I have a normal family where we discuss every detail of big stuff like Nal'Adel.

It's not as if I have a ton of other options.

Lady Cloake snaps her fingers again. The shadowy cage around us disappears. "No one dies today."

Turning, Lady Cloake starts over the bridge that leads to what I assume to be Nal'Adel's castle. *Good news.*

Ivy, however, is not pleased. "Wait!" She cries. "If you aren't going to kill Agatha, then why did you ask us to bring her here?"

Lady Cloake pauses and turns around. "Nal'Adel assumed she was an inferior human, but you never can be certain. I was instructed to check her, just in case." She gestures toward me. "And this thing is definitely powerless."

Ivy frowns. "Don't you think she might be hiding something under a glamour spell?"

Much as I hate to admit it, I have to give points here

to Ivy. While Marchesa avoids my presence, Ivy and I spend most of our days together. Clearly, she noticed something different about me.

"I have my orders," says Lady Cloake. "I have fulfilled them."

"But sometimes, Agatha looks like she has..." Ivy nibbles her lower lip.

"What's all this?" snaps Marchesa. "We discussed what would happen today. Oversharing about Agatha isn't part of the plan."

Lady Cloake tilts her head. "Sometimes it looks like she has *what?*"

"Like she has the ears of an elf," hisses Ivy. "Only for a second, though."

Marchesa gasps. "Ivy!"

"She's always wearing those hats, Mother. Don't you think it's strange?"

"There are many strange things about Agatha, but not her ears." Marchesa focuses on Lady Cloake. "You must excuse my daughter, we've been wandering the Faerie Lands for weeks now without food or shelter."

Lade Cloake stomps back in my direction. All of a sudden, it feels like my lungs are stuck in a vise. After pausing before me, Lady Cloake runs a clawed finger down my cheek. "Elf ears, eh?"

At this point, I could run, but that would be admitting that Ivy's telling the truth. The best thing I can do is stand here and try forcing air into my lungs.

Lady Cloake snaps her fingers. "We'll see."

Fresh shadow bindings rise up from the clouds to curl around me once again.

A tingle rises in my chest. *Oh, no.* My magic is awakening. Before, I wanted it so I could fight back. But in this moment, it will only serve to reveal my true nature.

Please, not now.

I make the mistake of glancing over to Ivy. Her face positively beams with joy.

"How empty you must feel," I whisper. "To need to fill yourself up on my pain." Ivy's smile melts away. *If I die now, at least I did that.*

Lady Cloake slides her clawed finger over my ear, pulling back my veil. She leans in until I sense her fetid breath along my throat.

Then she sinks her teeth into my flesh.

I cry out in surprise and shock. Pain spikes where her canines dig in. Blood trickles down my skin.

Lady Cloake leans away from me. For a long moment, she runs her long pointed tongue across her impossibly wide mouth.

I struggle against my shadow bindings, but they hold me too tightly. Panic zings through my limbs. What does

Lady Cloake plan to do next? Long seconds pass as she licks off every last drop of my blood.

"Human," declares Lady Cloake.

The shadow bindings vanish once more. I pull in long lungfuls of air. On reflex, I press my palm against the fresh wound on my throat.

Marchesa steps up to my side. "My dear sweet Agatha, are you all right?"

Here we go again. There's an audience, so I'm now *dear sweet Agatha.*

"I'm fine." And if my words have a bitter edge to them, so be it.

Normally, Ivy would play along with the display. Not this time. She steps closer to Lady Cloake. "Human?" asks Ivy. "Are you sure?"

"None but the Moonbeam King could cast a glamour spell to fool me, and he's been dead for many of your human years." Lady Cloake clacks her razor-sharp teeth together. "I am certain."

You'd think bleeding down my neck would be a shocker, but to me? These words from Lady Cloake are an even bigger deal. She just talked about the Moonbeam King. I'm definitely an elf, so my true self must be hidden by the power of the Moonbeam King. But why? How? And who does that make me, exactly?

I simply must find that mirror.

Ivy shakes her head. "Can't you check her one more time?"

I shoot Ivy an angry look. "Thanks for the support, *sister.*"

Lady Cloake rounds on Ivy. "I take orders from Nal'Adel alone. And my Mistress desires you to now visit Galloway Castle, the seat of Prince Jacoby. Once there, you shall proceed with the plan my Mistress has given you previously."

"But—" begins Ivy.

Lady Cloake snaps her fingers once more. Fresh shadow bindings rise up from the mist. Only this time, the ribbons surround Ivy.

Lady Cloake wags her clawed finger before Ivy's face. "I don't have any orders about your sorry hide. You can live or die, it's all the same to Nal'Adel. Do you know what that means?"

Ivy shakes her head.

"I could feast on your flesh right now. What do you say?" she stares at the pulse at Ivy's throat.

Maybe it's my fae side, but I know what will happen next. Ivy pushed Lady Cloake too far. My step-sister is about to become lunch.

There's no reason for me to speak up here. After all, Ivy just showed that she wouldn't do the same for me. Still, I won't let Marchesa and Ivy change me into someone who'll stand by and watch someone get chomped to death by a crazy elf... all when I could do something to stop it.

"Ivy is crucial to the great plan," I declare. "Nal'Adel will be displeased if you kill her."

Lady Cloake stares between me and Ivy, then she snaps her fingers once more. The bindings fall away. Without another word, Lady Cloake flies off toward the castle. This time, Ivy doesn't try to stop her.

Once we're alone again, Ivy and Marchesa yammer on about how I almost got them both killed. I ignore it. This happens every time I help my so-called family. With Ivy and Marchesa, I'm always the problem. Normally, I'd snap back and put them in their place.

Yet this time, I've bigger things to focus on.

Lady Cloake just ordered us all off to Prince Jacoby's palace. Just the thought makes my legs feel watery beneath me. In my mind, I picture Jacoby's aristocratic face. His hair is short, dark, and tousled while his body's lean and strong. Classic elf royalty.

That's not what's truly extraordinary about him, though. Jacoby wears determination like a suit of armor. No matter what, he forges ahead on everything with a sense of power and light.

I've had a crush on him since I can remember.

The prince has never noticed me though, only Elle.

Still, Jacoby is a royal in the fiefdom of Fortitude. If anyone knows where to find the Moonbeam Mirror, it will be him.

What if Jacoby and I went to find the mirror together? My stomach goes from just feeling fluttery into doing somersaults.

Calm down, Agatha.

I shake my head. Jacoby thinks about me as much as he would last weeks' bird's nest.

As we march closer to Galloway Castle, I keep reminding myself not to think about the prince. There's no way I can get caught up in romantic daydreams.

All that matters is finding that mirror.

7

JACOBY

GALLOWAY CASTLE

I loathe visiting my family's palaces; they're all drafty and full of ghosts.

Not metaphorical ones, mind you, such as the types who slam doors or go *boo* in the night. I'm talking real spirits with opinions that they insist on sharing. Overall, I find it's best to do my business here and return to Earth as quickly as possible. And when I do stay overnight in the Faerie lands, it's at a location no one knows.

That won't be the case today, though.

This morning, I walk the halls of Galloway Castle, the home of my late brother Frey. The purpose of my visit? I must cast a spell here that will confirm my new place in the line of succession. My companion for this unfortunate ritual is Doc Eight, a living suit of armor. He's what we Magicorum call an *animate*, meaning an object that gains magical consciousness.

While I march through the drafty stone passages, Doc lumbers along slowly behind me. I'm first to reach the heavy iron door that marks the entrance to today's unpleasantness.

Frey's throne room.

As I cross the threshold, one thing becomes obvious. The decor in here is horrible.

Frey had an unhealthy interest in anything bovine. My family rules an elven fiefdom called the Fortitude. Our magic powers such mighty creatures such as killer koi, megaphants and master kraken. We also dabble in Earthly beasts including rhinos and cows. All of these animals end up in our artwork. Frey simply went over-board in terms of bulls.

I step around in a slow circle. Massive horns adorn the walls. A great mosaic covers the floor, the colored tiles aligning into images of charging bulls. The throne itself is coated in a rather putrid brown hide. I'm assuming that's a bull skin, but with my family, you never know.

After a few minutes, Doc lumbers into the chambers, whereupon he immediately starts checking for booby traps. I allow him to inspect things, although I'd never have stepped foot inside this castle if my forecasting spell had detected any danger.

"The place is safe," declares Doc at last. Like always, his silver helm is kept in the *down* position. Doc is rather sensitive about his armor being empty inside.

"That's to be expected," I explain.

A gasp echoes through Doc's hollow self. "I disagree. The gates to this palace were wide open. No guards! I should think King Gorgan wants to keep his brother safe. After all, Gorgan is your oldest sibling. This could be even your new home, should you choose to take up residence here."

In truth, if Gorgan had sent guards here, it would be with orders to kill me. Not that I can explain such things right now. Elven walls have ears. Often literal ones.

Doc mistakes my silence for sadness. He shakes his head, a movement that lets off a series of metallic creaks. "What a grim day, your Highness."

"It should be," I reply.

It certainly was when my older brothers Abner, Barnaby, Cramley, Damascus and Edwin died.

"So it's not as melancholy this time?" asks Doc.

I shrug. "No one liked Frey. He smelled funny and spent far too much time with his cow herd. Frey also had a nasty habit of trying to assassinate his siblings."

"Did he..." Doc leaves the thought out there, but I

know what he's wondering. It's rare that I discuss my parents.

"The King and Queen essentially killed themselves." I shoot him a look that says, *and that's all I'm saying about this point.*

Doc clears his throat, which is one of his ways of changing the subject.

An excellent idea.

"I can't believe it," Doc continues. "You're now fourth in line for the royal throne of Fortitude."

"Don't remind me," I state. "My family has a dismal record when it comes to life span. Now only Gorgan, Harold, and..." I snap my fingers, trying to remember the name.

"Prince Ignatius."

"Right. Now only Gorgan, Harold, and Ignatius stand in line before me." I step closer to the very pungent throne. "Ah, well. Best to get it over with."

Now that Frey is dead, it's time to announce my new status in the line of succession. Doc is right that I could also take over his home. I won't, though.

I take my seat on the stinky throne. All I need to do now is recline here while saying a spell. After that, I shall return to Earth before I'm poisoned, shredded, or otherwise destroyed.

Leaning back my head, I pull on my inner power.

The room darkens. An electric sense of magic crackles in the air. "I, Prince Jacoby of the Fortitude, do hereby acknowledge my new place in the line of accession." I glance around the chamber. I could state that I own this castle as well, but I won't add that in. No point getting magically tied to anything if you can avoid it. Who knows what curses have been laid on these walls?

"Is that everything?" asks Doc. He knows there's a long version of this particular speech. To begin with, I have about twelve separate names and titles that I could add into the mix, including how my family is aligned to the Unseelie Fae, what humans call dark elves. But both the Unseelie and Seelie courts have been gone for years. There's no one left to be offended if I skip that part.

"We're doing the short version today," I reply. "And thus endeth the spell." The room lightens. All sense of power fades from the air.

Time to return to Earth.

Speaking of the human realm, I still need to find a powerful wife to help keep me alive. Elle remains my top choice. She's a warden of magic, nice to look at, and not yet wed to that Alec fellow. And, most importantly, I really don't care if she lives or dies.

That's the ticket to staying alive in the Faerie Lands: *pleasant detachment.*

Emotional entanglements are only a horrid waste of

good energy. Other elves see your affection as weakness. And they're right. In short order, those feelings will be used to murder you in any number of ways.

Mother always said that she'd rather drink poison than fall in love. Both cause your death, yet only poison allows you to set the time and place.

A wise woman, my mother. That is, until she and father decided to help the Unseelie fight a pointless war.

Suddenly, one wall of the chamber becomes swathed in shadow. A door appears in the darkness.

Doc turns toward me, a motion that lets off a fresh chorus of squeaking noises. "Do we fight?"

"No," I reply. "We wait."

A fae door appears in the darkness. It swings open; Lady Cloake steps through.

"Milady," I state. "Good to see you."

Which is a lie. It's outrageous that someone can simply walk into my throne room. Yet if I act like it's a breach of my security, I'll look weak. So I fake pleasant greetings on the outside. Meanwhile, my heart stays happy that I'll never have to live in Galloway Castle. This place is about as warded as a brick of Swiss cheese.

She tears off her mouth. "The Mistress of Moon-shadow requests your presence."

That's Lady Cloake for you. She's all business. As

mercenaries go, this fae is very efficient. Still, in this case, she won't be effective.

"As you can see, I'm on my throne. Nal'Adel can enter *my* castle."

The politics behind this is that my fiefdom has an opposite in power, namely the Miniscule. Their magic enhances all members of the Fortitude and vice-versa.

Unlike Nal'Adel.

The Mistress of Moonshadow doesn't have a Mistress of Moonbeams. All of which means that Nal'Adel must understand her place in the power structure.

"I will relay your message." Lady Cloake stalks back through the fae door. A moment later, Nal'Adel enters my throne room. She's as lovely and deadly as ever.

"Greetings, Prince Jacoby."

"Mistress Nal'Adel."

"I visit today with important information. There's a prophecy that I will find my Mistress of Moonbeams."

"That *is* news."

In all honestly, you can't swing a dead troll without hitting a prophecy in the Faerie Lands. But when it comes to antagonizing Nal'Adel, I must pick my battles.

"Shall I recite it?" she asks.

"Please do."

Nal'Adel closes her eyes. When she speaks, her voice has an ethereal, sing-song quality.

> One who channels the power of moonlight
> Hides on Earth in dark
> She knows nothing of her true magic
> Until the Mistress of Moonbeams calls the mark.

After opening her eyes, Nal'Adel refocuses on me. "Well, what do you think?"

"It's an interesting prophecy," I say blandly.

"I think I have found the human who is described in this prophecy. My Mistress of Moonbeams is Elle Cynder."

Shock zings through my body, but I fight the urge to show any reaction. Nal'Adel must not suspect that I have any true feelings toward Elle. Doing so would be the equivalent of handing my enemy a sword and hoping they don't kill me.

"I plan to hold a great party," continues Nal'Adel. "The humans call it a Glass Slipper Ball. I think you could be the prince for this celebration. Do you agree? Or would that threaten your sweet Elle Cynder too much?"

At this point, saying *no* would essentially place an even larger target on Elle's back. To Nal'Adel, Elle must be just some human that I toy with.

Which she is. The fact that I'm gripping this foul throne with such force, my fingers dig into the wood? That's simply a coincidence. I don't get attached to anyone, least of all Elle.

Still, I take a long moment to size up Nal'Adel's reaction. The woman's antennae-like brows twitch with anticipation. She's more invested in this new Glass Slipper Ball than she wants me to know.

All of which means one thing.

"You've already announced this, haven't you?" I ask.

"Only a little."

I roll my eyes. "Really."

"All right, I've said quite a bit. There are layers of plans on this; you can't expect me to explain them all. What do you say? Keep your enemies closer and archenemies closer?"

Nal'Adel is right on that score. If I refuse, Nal'Adel will just find another prince to use at the ball. And I can't protect Elle if I'm not there. *Not that I'd protect Elle anyway.* Although in all honestly, I probably will.

Being an evil elf is rather confusing sometimes.

"Of course," I reply. "I have no ties on this score."

Nal'Adel sighs. "Perfect. I'll let you know your orders soon."

I rise. "No one orders me."

"My mistake," says Nal'Adel quickly. "Lady Cloake will find you and deliver our joint plans in due time."

I retake my throne. "Much better."

With that, Nal'Adel steps off through the fae door. Within seconds, the shadows recede and the wall is back to normal.

Fresh knocks sound at the chamber's real wooden door. I hadn't realized Doc had closed us in. It's a wise choice, though.

"Shall I check the door, my Prince?"

"Please do."

Since Doc scoped things out, he knows the chamber walls hold hidden peepholes. Doc marches right over to the closest one. He really is extraordinarily efficient. I couldn't ask for more in a servant. Doc even pretends to be my boss when we are hiding out on earth. That isn't easy, once you know who I truly am.

Doc removes an obliging bull horn from the wall. A small hole sits in the plaster. Doc looks through. "You have a group outside who wishes to speak with you."

"Assassins?"

"Not exactly."

Stepping down from my throne, I use the peep hole myself. A rather ragtag group waits in the outer hall. It's Marchesa, Agatha, Ivy, Diamond and Legend. I'd heard they'd been pardoned from Queen of Hearts dungeon.

So long as they are in the Faerie Lands, they may remain free.

I roll my eyes. Elle and Alec are really too soft-hearted, pardoning them all like that. *Ah, well.* If Elle becomes my bride, I'll have to educate her on the uses of sympathy. As in, there are none.

I reset the bull horn into its spot in the wall.

Doc tilts his metal helm. It's his silent way of asking. *Do you wish to see them?*

I'm about to say, *never,* but then I sense it.

A pulse of power.

In fact, it's the very magical signature I detected in Elle's bedroom. It's elvish and of unknown origin. I retake my stinky throne.

"Allow them in," I command.

The pack of supplicants spill into the room. Legend seems to be the self-appointed leader.

"We heard you'd returned to the Faerie Lands," says Legend. "We wished to see you."

It's an effort not to roll my eyes again. "Obviously."

Marchesa sashays forward. "I hope you won't resent how we treated you back on Earth. We'd no idea who you really were."

Legend continues. "Imagine our surprise when we're released from the queen's dungeons, thinking we don't have a friend in the Faerie Lands. Then we discover who you really are!"

I sigh. "Is there a request you wish to make? Because this is taking way too long."

"We want our lives back," says Legend. "Diamond and I want to rule over Le Charme Jewelers forever. Marchesa and her daughters desire their station restored at Cynder Mercantile. And we all need gold to support ourselves."

"And what do you offer in return?"

Marchesa strides forward. She pulls a small container from the folds of her cloak. "I can offer you this: the Coffer of Wonders. It could be aligned to the dark elves and give you whatever you need that day."

Interesting. "Show me."

Marchesa opens the box. There's a small puff of smoke, followed by a scrap of paper flying out of the container. I pluck the tiny document from the air. "This provides the address for Kokkivo."

"Yes," confirms Marchesa. "No doubt, the coffer wishes us to bring the phoenix back to Cynder Mercantile."

"Does the coffer do such things often?"

"Absolutely," answers Marchesa. "The coffer offers excellent advice."

"And sometimes, it even provides a nice luncheon,"

adds Legend. "Isn't that right?"

"So delicious," confirms Marchesa.

I crumple the paper and drop it to the floor. "That's rather limited, isn't it? More bossy than actual help."

Legend lifts his chin. "We can offer you other things."

"Name it," I state.

Legend bows low. "You'd have a promise of our eternal loyalty."

I laugh. "Not acceptable."

Once more, that pulse of power moves through the room. This time, the source is easily discerned.

Agatha.

Stepping down from my throne, I cross the floor and approach the girl. Like always, she wears a boxy dress and large veil. I stop before her.

"Remove the veil, please."

Agatha does nothing. It isn't something that comes from fear. No, this girl's got fight in her. Clearly, Agatha doesn't like being ordered around. The waves of elven power turn even more intense. I scan the other faces nearby. They can't detect a thing.

Who is this girl?

Moving closer, I take care to gentle my voice. "Please."

Agatha removes both her veil. She has an aristocratic face with wise dark eyes. Long waves of brown hair cascade down her back. I reach forward and slide some strands behind her ear. The feel of her skin sends a pleasant jolt through my chest. And my touch reveals something even more exciting.

No question about it. The tips of her ears point upwards. Agatha is an elf.

"I want them safe and taken care of," she whispers. I scan the room. No one else heard her words.

Again, I wonder. Who is this girl?

I retake my throne. "I have reconsidered. Elle and Alec aren't married yet. For my own reasons, I wish to break up that relationship. Am I right in assuming we share that goal?"

"Oh, yes," gushes Legend. "That's exactly what we want!"

"What is your plan?" asks Marchesa. "What can we do to help?"

"You can remain here in the Faerie Lands and stay out of my way. But I do need your consent that I take one of your daughters back with me to the human realm. Consider it a sign of your support."

"Of course," says Marchesa. "You have my agreement. Both my daughters are yours."

A small grin rounds my mouth. Marchesa should never agree so quickly to anything with a resident of the Faerie Lands. I speak a single word. "Perfect."

"You'll take Ivy with you, of course." Marchesa pushes her eldest daughter forward. "If you wish to break up Elle and Alec, Ivy is the one to do it."

"I'll take Agatha," I state.

"What?" Marchesa gasps. "You must take Ivy."

"I must do whatever I want. You already promised both your daughters to me. " I crook my finger toward Agatha.

A smile quirks the girl's mouth as she slips closer. "You have a request for me?"

A request. She even talks like a royal.

"Yes," I state. "How do you fancy working in an Earth store with me and Doc Eight?" I tap my chin. "On second thought, don't bother answering. You're going with me. Now."

With the blink of an eye, I cast a spell to transport me, Doc, and Agatha out of Galloway Castle.

I haven't been this intrigued in years.

And that stuff about returning to Earth? All lies. I'd rather be torn apart in the wild hunt than tell those fools my true plans. No question about it. Legend, Diamond, Marchesa and Ivy are in league with Nal'Adel. Agatha is a wild card, though.

Can this evil stepsister be more useful to me than her Cinderella?

I'll find out soon enough.

8

ELLE

ONE WEEK LATER

*I*t's another early morning with my enchanted stalkers and wizard boyfriend. Alec and I have our regular places for this ritual. He's seated on his favorite chair; I'm camped out by the bedroom window. And the stalkers? They're playing their part as well.

"Elle! Elle! We want Cinderella!"

Noisy little buggers.

Across the bedroom, Alec flips to a new page in his notebook. "What do you have for me today?"

"Thirty-one humans are traipsing around down there. Twelve carry signs. Each one reads the same thing as always. *Pick a new prince, Elle!*"

Alec scribbles on the sheet before him. "They're not a very creative group, are they? Sure there's nothing else?"

Turning, I inspect the crowd once more. "Oh, I missed one. A new sign reads, *Choose...*" I squint, not believing what I'm seeing. "*Prince Jacoby!*"

"What. The. Hell." Alec leaps up, runs over to the window and scans the sidewalk below. "That's what it says, all right."

This is rather unexpected, to say the least. Jacoby is an eighteen-year-old elf hottie and my long-time buddy. Sadly, the man simply doesn't understand the concept of *friend zone*. The last time I saw Jacoby was right before the Glass Slipper Ball. At that point, he suggested that we merge our powers and futures. For the millionth time, I told him *no*.

"Have you heard from Jacoby since the ball?" asks Alec.

"Not a peep. Even so, this new sign is definitely *not* from him."

"How can you be sure?"

"If Jacoby wanted something, he'd just show up and ask." I point toward the window. "Whoever made that sign? They want us to *think* it's Jacoby."

"You're right." Alec presses his palms against his eyes. "And this stuff is connected somehow, I can feel it."

"Well, all those enchanted humans work at the same place in the Village."

My very special stalkers all work at a spot called the old Bazaar—it's an outdoor faire that runs on weekends. Alec and I looked into every employee and which tent they worked. Beyond the fact that they were employed at the same place, we couldn't find any patterns.

Alec shakes his head. "It's more than where they work. I just can't put my finger on it."

I hug my elbows. "I agree."

This situation with my stalkers is like those blown up drawings made of tiny little dots. Up close, it's a bunch of nonsense. It's only when you step back far enough that you can see an actual picture. Trouble is, both Alec and I have been at this for weeks. We still have no idea of a bigger pattern.

All of a sudden, a fresh round of chants echo into the apartment. "Lost her wings! Lost her wings! Sad little fairy has lost her wings!"

I glance over to Alec. *Did he hear that?* Based on the mixture of outrage and empathy in his eyes, he certainly did. What else would I expect? Whatever magic protects humans from detecting my enchanted stalkers, it doesn't affect Magicorum like Alec.

On reflex, I rub at my shoulders, right at the place

where my wings should be. There's nothing. Once again, my soul cracks with sorrow.

Alec crosses the room to pull me into a deep hug. When he next speaks, his voice is a soothing purr. "You're perfect, just as you are."

Shaking my head, I try to toss thoughts of my lost wings from my mind. Not happening. "I feel them sometimes, Alec. It's like I can fly away, but when I look, there's nothing on my back but scars."

Alec kisses the top of my head. "I'm so sorry."

I sniffle and reorganize myself. "I've got this. Who cares if random humans stalk my sidewalk? Why worry that the Colonel took away my best friend on a secret adventure? And how can I get upset about some lost wings?" When I ask that last question, my voice breaks with grief.

Alec pulls me in closer; I lean more deeply into his hug. "Was that an internal pep talk?"

"Yeah." I sigh. "Not too good, eh?"

Alex leans back until our gazes lock. "Here's what's going to happen. We'll both get ready for school. Then I'll transport you to West Lake Prep in time for class."

I frown. "But you have some kind of torture festival going on today. You're not supposed to be at school."

"Yes, I'm leading the annual board meeting for Le Charme industries this morning. But if we leave soon,

I'll have more than enough time to get you to school *and* meet with the board."

"Thank you." I force a smile. "And like always, I'll be ready in twenty."

"That's my Elle."

Alec steps away, reaches into his pocket and pulls out a huge sapphire. He raises the gemstone, then pauses. Alec's gaze locks with mine.

"Whatever is happening with those stalkers, I know one thing. You *will* figure it out." All the love I've ever known shines in Alec's eyes. "I have total faith in you, Elle."

At those words, something deep within me awakens. A buzz of power moves through my chest. I felt this before, but never so strongly. It's my own fae magic. A sense of knowing and rightness ignites my very soul.

"Yes," I say solemnly. "I believe I will."

Alec lifts his fist and creates a pillar of blue light. A moment later, Alec is gone. His words stay with me, though.

You will *figure it out.*

For a minute, I pace my bedroom and think through my options.

An idea appears.

And I love the concept.

Sure, my transport spell had me arriving at home

naked, but I did get here. Why should I wait around for some enchanted humans to let me know what's wrong with my life? I can cast my own spell and get the truth. No more looking through windows.

Alec called it. I *will* find the answers I need.

And I'll do it right now.

9

ELLE

*N*ow I talk a big game about casting a divining spell, but I stall a little bit before I start.

Okay, I stall a lot.

In my defense, I do need a snack. There's also the fact that I'm two levels behind Alec on our favorite game, Magicorum Killers. So I have to focus on that for a little while. Eventually, I run out of things to pretend that I need to do. It's time to get magical.

One spell, coming right up.

Closing my eyes, I tap into the power inside my chest. Energy zings through my limbs. The pulse of magic grows stronger within me. I raise my arms; pink light erupts around me. A haze of sparkling fairy dust congeals by my hands.

Pure joy sparks in my heart. I've never tapped into this much magic before. Next, I need to focus it. Beyond boiling water, I haven't mastered any complex spells yet. In all honesty, I'm not sure what comes next.

So I make stuff up.

"Oh, my magic," I begin. "Send me some help so I can figure out what's happening with these human stalkers." Since that sounds a little abrupt, I decide to add a little more to my incantation. "That is, if you're not busy. Thank you."

My fairy dust now expands into a tall cloud of all things pink and sparkly. When the spell ends, the fairy dust vanishes. In its place, Sky is here.

"Hello, there," she says in a drawl. "I'm Skye." She snaps her fingers and her legs transform into a puff of smoke. "I'm a genie."

Oh, no.

In the world of Magicorum, there are two phrases you don't want to hear: *The magical rapture is nigh* and *hello, I'm a genie.*

At this point, I'd prefer the rapture.

"Nice to officially meet you, Skye. I do remember you from my classroom and everything." I shoot her a little wave. "Thanks for stopping by, but you can just mosey along now. Please don't take this the wrong way, but I summoned you by mistake."

Skye drops into a crouch and proceeds to do one of those Russian kick dance things for a minute straight, all while crying out, "cock-a-doodle-doo!"

My heart sinks. *What the hell have I gotten myself into?*

Finally, Skye stops her kick fest. "Summoning me wasn't a mistake. You meant to pull me here for one simple reason: you're turning into a genie yourself. You're *dissolving.*"

"Whatever. I am not turning into a genie." This isn't my best comeback, but it's early in the morning and I wasn't expecting a genie in my bedroom.

"Really?" asks Skye. "What's the first sign that you're dissolving?" While she waits for my answer, Skye sets her hands under armpits and flaps like a bird.

Oh man, was this ever a bad idea.

"I'm waiting." Skye now adds a jutting head motion to her bird impression. Combined with the fact that her hat is tall and round, she reminds me of Bert from Sesame Street as he does a pigeon impression.

Shoot me now.

Still, I answer her question. "The first sign is that you think you have two fairy tale life templates. But that's not me."

"Is it? You're a thief, aren't you?"

"Only because my stepfamily really sucks." *Which is true.*

"And the stalker humans out there... didn't you find out that they all work in the same place?"

"Yeah, they're from an outdoor shopping faire."

Skye stops her pigeon dance. "And what's that place called?"

"The Old Bazaar." The moment the words leave my mouth, I can see where Skye is going with this.

"Let's count up the Aladdin references here." Skye rubs her hands together. "First there's you, the thief. Second, your stalkers work at the Old Bazaar, a place where Aladdin did some serious stealing. And third, there's me, your genie. You can kid yourself but you can't fool me. You're dissolving from a Cinderella life template into one that's about Aladdin. Soon, you'll be a genie, same as I am." She sets her hand under her armpit again, only this time it's to make fart noises.

And this is why I never, ever want to become a genie. Fart noises? Seriously?

"What do you say?" asks Skye. "Want to take the plunge and become a genie?"

"Ah, no." Again, that's not a great comeback but I'm doing my best here.

"But it's so lovely to be a genie. You meet people. Fly around. Cast spells. Live alone for eternity." She floats up to sit on the ceiling. "It does get lonesome, by the way. You get used to it, though." She rolls her eyes in opposite direction at the same time while singing the Oscar Meyer Weiner song.

I pinch the bridge of my nose. "Why couldn't I get a genie that does celebrity impersonations? This is a disaster."

"No, I'll tell you what's a disaster. Nal'Adel, the Mistress of Moonshadow. She's the one behind your human stalkers. There, I did what your spell commanded and gave you some answers."

It's true that genies are unhinged. But they're also unable to lie. So whatever this news is about Nal'Adel, it's important. "Tell me more."

"You know how it works in Faerie Lands. The place is a ton of little fiefdoms fighting it out for power." Skye raises her right hand and makes it talk like a puppet.

"I want power," says Skye's right hand.

"No, I want power," says her left.

"You follow?" asks Skye.

It would be easier if she weren't using hand puppets while sitting on my ceiling, but I won't get picky right now. "Sure, I understand."

"And every fiefdom comes in pairs. Summer and Winter. East and West. Seelie and Unseelie. Get it?"

"Sure do."

"Well, Nal'Adel is the Mistress of Moonshadow. Only her opposite, the Mistress of Moonbeams, has never appeared. You can imagine why that's a problem."

"Actually, I can't."

"Having an opposite feeds your power. Paired fief-doms steal magic back and forth. Being without your other half cuts your potential power base in half." Now Skye starts flying around my bedroom like it's a race track. I give her a minute to get her yayas out before I interrupt.

"So what does Nal'Adel want with me?"

Skye stops. "For years, Nal'Adel has had agents out searching for the Mistress of Moonbeams. At the Glass Slipper Ball, one of them detected a unique magical signature on you. Now Nal'Adel thinks you're her missing half. And you know what happens next, don't you?"

"She wants me to move to the Faerie Lands and share power?"

Skye laughs so hard, she does aerial somersaults around the room. "No, silly. She wants to drain your magic. These enchanted humans are only the beginning. Nal'Adel will use them and other tools in order to herd you someplace where she can destroy you, body and soul. Ta ta!"

"No," I cry. "Wait! We were just getting to the useful stuff."

But Skye is gone.

I try summoning the genie again. Nothing happens. In fact, I'm so focused on my task that I don't even notice how Alec is back.

"Elle, are you okay?"

Sure, I could tell the truth here. But it would be the oldest cliche in the book. The first thing anyone who's dissolving says is that a genie told them they're dissolving... but that will never happen.

There's no way I'm sharing any of this with Alec right now. I need to think through how to position this properly. Alec has enough to worry about without thinking I'm going cuckoo, genie-style.

"Don't worry, Alec. I'm totally fine."

"But you're still in your pajamas. I was going to transport you to school, remember?"

"Right. Oops. I'll get ready in a jiffy."

In the end, I get dressed in all of ninety seconds. Fast costume changes are a necessary part of being a con artist. In short order, I'm wearing a brown dress and sandals. And did I mention that Alec wears a suit coat and fancy shirt? He does. Yum yum.

I slap on what I hope is a convincing smile. "Ready!"

Alec gives me the side-eye. "Maybe you'll tell me what's really happening over dinner tonight?"

My forced grin turns into a real one. It's wonderful to have someone like Alec in my life. The man understands me deeply.

"Yes," I reply. "I absolutely will."

ALEC

7:26 AM
   I just dropped off Elle at school. Now I'm back in the board room of the famous Le Charme Building in Midtown Manhattan. As usual, I stand at the head of the table and close to the exit.

Today, the room is packed with old white guys who sit at high-back chairs. *All human.* The only one I've ever met before is the Duke. Still, all these guys glare at me like they're certain I need a binky and a nap.

I get it, folks. You're unhappy that I'm eighteen and running the company. Time to move on.

I glance at the clock. 7:29AM

The old dudes keep staring. It's an art form to hold all their gazes at once, but I manage to do it. This is my way of saying, *I'm not just any magic user, boys. I'm the warden of all witch and warlock power.*

One by one, they all look away.

I call that a win.

7:30 AM

"It is time," announces the Duke.

"Thank you."

After I slip off my suit coat, I set the garment onto the back of my chair. It's another part of my regular routine.

As I make this movement, a low chorus of gasps sounds around the room. For their part, the board remains buttoned up. Clearly, they aren't used to the idea of *business casual*. Even so, based on the shocked gazes, you'd think I just stripped down to a mankini or something.

Oh, well. They'll adjust.

I rub my palms together. "Let's start with the new WebWorld contract." I hold up my phone. "I've been coming to this building since I was a toddler, and I have yet to get consistent phone or internet. Things must be fixed before I sign a renewal."

The Duke clears his throat. "With all due respect, my Prince Alec, there's another topic that we need to discuss. We need your approval on something far more critical than that interwebs contract."

"It's called the internet. And what's more important, in your opinion?"

"The new Glass Slipper Ball."

I do a double-take. "The *what*? There's just one Glass Slipper Ball, and it happened when I turned eighteen. If I get married and have a son and *he* turns eighteen, then we can talk about another ball. But until then? It's on hold. Back to internet access, people."

"We disagree." The Duke snaps his fingers.

The main door opens. A troop of employees in fancy livery stroll in. Each one carries a binder that's thick as a brick. Moving in unison, they set the massive black volumes onto the tabletop, one binder for each of us.

The Duke taps the huge item before him. "This holds all the details." He snaps his fingers once more. The guy behind me opens my binder to the last page and hands me an old-timey quill pen.

The Duke tries to smile, but it comes off as more of a snarl. "Just sign that last page and we can move on to… whatever mumbo jumbo you want to discuss."

I turn the quill over in my hands. As a master wizard, I know when someone hands me an enchanted pen. Whatever I sign with this thing will be magically binding for all eternity.

In a pointed move, I set the quill onto the tabletop. "What's this all about?"

"I don't know what you mean." The Duke scans the other faces around the table. "Do you, my friends?"

In reply, there's a lot of head-shaking and false smiles. The Duke is such the ringleader here. I need to fix that, soon.

I pull my suit coat back on. My jacket may look like a regular human piece of clothing, but in reality? It's packed with the magical stones I use in order to cast spells.

Important side note. I'm not a fan of the *man bags* most wizards carry around. You can just as easily enchant a sport coat to carry supplies, and there's the added bonus of *not* looking like you fell out of a bad version of *Lord of the Rings*.

Reaching into my pocket, I pull out a massive ruby. This thing is so loaded with magic, it almost buzzes against my palm. Rubies are best for truth-telling incantations. Based on the wide eyes around the room, I'm guessing these guys know that fact as well.

I hold the gemstone high. "You *will* tell me what this is about, whether you want to or not. The Duke here is warded against spells, but the rest of you are fair game." I round on my chairman. "How about you spare your fellow board members some pain and just volunteer what's going on?"

The Duke glares at me, his milky eyes overflowing

with hatred. "Your parents set up another Glass Slipper Ball."

I sniff. "If they did, they never told me."

"Perhaps if you hadn't sent your parents off into exile, they could have given you an update."

The way the Duke snarls out those words, you'd think I was being an asshat for exiling my parents because *they tortured me.*

I lower my voice. "How about *you* tell me *now?*"

"Glass Slipper Balls are great for showing off our jewels," answers the Duke. "Your parents wanted to start having them regularly to drive sales. The next one is planned to take place one week from today."

I bob my head, considering. As plans go, this is pretty solid. Still, it's totally odd that this news was hidden from me. There must be a catch.

"Who's the lucky prince?" I ask. "Because I'm already taken, thank you very much."

Yet even as I ask the question, I'm fairly certain of the answer. It was written on a sign outside Elle's window this morning.

The Duke lifts his chin. "A royal elf named Jacoby. He attends your high school."

"And it will be a masquerade ball this time," adds another random old guy. "We're refurbishing the L Center as we speak."

The Duke gestures toward my quill. "How about you go ahead and sign?"

"Not until I've read this thoroughly." I push the binder aside. "Which I'll do later."

"But my Prince Alec, we were planning to have you sign this now. There are contractors that must get approvals. It could delay the event for months." The Duke shivers. "You know we need help with revenue."

I pause, considering this. The Duke is right that our sales are in the toilet. But I'm more concerned about what's really going on with this Glass Slipper Ball. With a binder this huge, there's bound to be some clues hidden within. And considering how anxious my board is for me to sign? Waiting might get them to blab a few secrets.

No question about it. I need to review this binder, make up a list of questions, and press these guys for answers, fast.

"Here's what I can do," I begin. "We'll move *the Glass Slipper Ball pow wow* to next week. I'll take a look at everything in the meantime. But expect me to return with questions and not an enchanted quill. Another Glass Slipper Ball is a big deal. I must understand everything before signing."

"As you command," says the Duke. "The meeting is adjourned." Everyone starts to rise.

"Not so fast," I counter. "I said *the Glass Slipper Part* of the meeting, not everything. I still want to go through a bunch of other stuff, including that WebWorld contract."

"Are you certain that can't wait as well?" asks the Duke.

"Positive. If something isn't signed today, our employees will have no internet access. To me, that's far more important than a ball."

The old guys stay frozen in a crouch that's halfway between standing upright and retaking their seats. All of them stare at the Duke.

I snap my fingers. "Don't look to the Duke; I'm your CEO. Park your bony butts and let's get to work."

So that's what we do.

All the while, I ask for copies of every odd document that crosses the table. My goal? Find more stuff like the surveillance report from the mysterious L. Cloake.

It's going to be a long day.

11

ELLE

School started off great, mostly because Alec dropped me off again. *Yay, Alec!*

Right now, I'm hanging in homeroom. To kill time, I run through today's schedule in my head. We fae loathe routine. Every day is different. Here's what I've got coming up.

7:37:23AM. Homeroom.

Key fact. Fae classes start at times that are either incredibly exact or super sketchy. It's how we roll.

9AM-ish. *Spell Casting for Dummies* class. This is my daily nightmare with Miss Morningdew.

10:30AM-ish. Open discussion. This is another way of saying that everyone hangs out and socializes. I wait in the back and *wing watch*.

12:01:17PM. Lunch. Pixies can conjure you something to eat, but I watch those little buggers when no one else is paying attention. They totally spit on everything. I bring my own food, thank you very much.

1PM-ish. Assembly and an inspirational speech from our Principal Goldilocks. This fae carries around an especially sloppy lollipop which she wields like a conductor's baton. If you sit in the first two rows at assembly, expect to get splattered in yuck. Again, I hang in the back.

2:15:14PM. *How to Manipulate Humans* class. Self-explanatory and when you're me, pretty useless.

3PM-ish. Closing meeting. We discuss homework and whatnot.

I decide to kill even more time and text Alec. For once, his phone works inside the Le Charme Building.

CallMeElle: meet @ my place after school? lots 2 tell u

MagicMan: Sure

Alec accents his point by sending me a gif of dancing yetis. The guy downloads internet memes that match my pajama collection. Does he know me or what?

CallMeElle: hehe

MagicMan: lots 2 tell u 2

After that text exchange, I sleepwalk through the day. I may look like I'm just sulking in the back of the classroom, but I'm really thinking through that conversation with Skye and worrying about Alec. Finally, school ends and I speed my way home. Fortunately, I remembered my *Plus-Ten Cloak Of Hiding.* In no time, I'm in my kitchen and making myself a sandwich-asaurus when some familiar blue sparkles shine out from the living room.

Alec is here.

Because I'm just an awesome girlfriend, I cut my sandwich-asaurus in half and head over to the couch. The moment I close in on Alec, one thing is very clear.

"What's up with the binder?"

Alec chuckles. "This thing holds the plans for the next Glass Slipper Ball."

"No. Way."

"You go first, though. What's your news?"

This morning, I was too shocked about meeting a genie to blab about the experience. Since then, I've had all day to obsess over Skye. I'm totally ready to share.

"So," I begin. "I summoned a genie."

"You did what?"

"Me. A girl genie. It happened."

"Wow. Do you have any idea how tough that is to do?"

"Not really. At school, we just finished learning how to use fairy dust in order to boil water. It was harder than that, definitely."

"Tell me about her."

"Her name is Skye and—" I close my eyes and just plow through this next bit of news "—she thinks I'm dissolving into a genie myself."

Alec frowns. "Where does she get that from?"

"Skye claims there's a lot of Aladdin going on in my life." I count the signs on my fingers. "One, I'm a thief. Two, my stalkers are from the Old Bazaar. Three, I summoned a genie."

I set my snack aside. Now that I'm talking genie stuff with Alec, I'm not so hungry anymore. For a long minute, Alec only stares at me. Normally, the guy is a pretty open book. But now? I can't tell what he's thinking at all. Is he shocked? Angry? Ready to eat his sandwich and move on?

At last, Alec breaks the silence. "Hmm."

"That's it? Hmm?"

"I won't say that Skye is wrong about the Aladdin thing. You are a bit of a thief and scoundrel."

"Thanks."

He chuckles. "And that's what I'm talking about.

Most people wouldn't be happy to be called those things."

"I'm a *little* unusual."

"I noticed." He winks. "And it's a good thing."

My heart sinks. "So you think I'm doomed to become a genie?"

"I don't think anyone could make you do anything unless it met your own desires."

All day long, I'd been carrying the weight of this news. And just like that, Alec's words relieve the pressure from my soul. "Thanks again."

"Any time."

Now my snack is looking mighty tempting. "So tell me about your day." I slide the plate closer.

Alec explains how the board sprung this Glass Slipper Ball on him... Why the binder may hold clues about what's really going on... And that next week will be the time to get any questions answered.

"It all adds up to one thing," Alec concludes. "My parents have found an ally in the Faerie Lands."

"And if someone is helping your family then, let's face it, Marchesa and friends won't be far behind."

"Agreed."

I remember what Alec told me about the surveillance reports. "Did you find out anything new about L. Cloake?"

"No, and I cast a ton of knowledge spells about it, too. I keep running into protection spells that block me, though. Whoever this L. Cloake is, she has some serious magic behind her."

"And the binder? Did you cast knowledge spells on that thing, too?"

"I did. Same result. This binder is covered in rock-solid protection. The only way to review it is by human means."

"So we need to go through it, word for word."

Alec grins. "We?"

"Hey, we're both in this, right? With a Glass Slipper Ball in the mix, this is looking more and more like a Cinderella template problem. Color me happy. Not that I was worried about fading into an Aladdin life and going cuckoo. Much."

At this point, I realize I may be babbling just a little bit, so I bite my lips together, hard.

Alec gives me the side-eye. "I told you, Elle. No one can make you do or be anything"

"Well, I want to be who I am, right now. And that's someone with a lot of reading to do."

"And on the plus side, we can order delivery tonight. Ronnie's Pizza?"

"My favorite." I raise my pointer finger. "And one more item."

"What?"

"When this board meeting happens, I'm going with you."

Alec gives me one of his most dazzling smiles. "You're perfect, Elle."

I make a kissy face at him. "I know."

With that, Alec and I launch through hours of pouring through the smallest type you've ever seen. Sadly, the pages are both out of order and not numbered, so our first task is figuring out what goes where.

By the time 1AM rolls around, we've found the first twenty-seven pages. Only a thousand more to go.

This is going to take a while.

JACOBY'S GARDEN

12

AGATHA

One second, I'm shivering inside Jacoby's castle. The next moment, I stand in a country garden. Warm breezes caress my skin. Jacoby waits nearby. As so often happens with this guy, his features are both handsome and unreadable.

"You said we're headed for Earth," I declare.

"True. Your listening skills are commendable."

What a sarcastic ass. Well, I never backed down from Marchesa or Ivy. I certainly won't start groveling to Jacoby.

"Guess what? I also have the power of observation." I shoot Jacoby a look that encompasses a single idea: *duh.* "We're still in the Faerie Lands."

"Whatever makes you say that?"

"This place is too lovely." A thought appears. The

instant the idea hits my mind, I know that it's the truth. "This is your secret home."

If my words shock Jacoby, he doesn't show it. "Perhaps."

"And you've magically protected it from predators, too. Nal'Adel can't get to us here, can she?"

Jacoby sighs. "You're tiresome."

"I'm also right."

Jacoby steps closer. "So I've noticed." His dark eyes reflect the rising moon in strange ways. My stomach twists with an emotion I don't know how to name. Something comes alive in my chest—it's that unsettling buzz which means my magic is on the move.

All of a sudden, a patch of moonlight appears on a nearby path.

Then it rises.

The moonbeam congeals into a pulsing ball. A name appears in my mind. *Will-o-the-wisp.* These lead travelers off their chosen trails and into danger.

Part of me screams that I should run in the opposite direction. No question about it; will-o-the-wisps are bad news. But more of me is entranced by what looks like a tiny moon.

The will-o-the-wisp races off.

I follow.

The world around me turns hazy. My body goes

numb. I speed through a maze of looming trees and tall hedges, my feet easily finding a path where there should be none. All the while, I keep my arms outstretched, ready to catch the will-o-the-wisp. No matter what I do, it stays out of reach.

Although I'm mostly blocked off from the world, I'm still vaguely aware that Jacoby trails behind me, calling out my name. I can't seem to make myself care, though. The will-o-the-wisp is so bright and perfect. If I could just hold it, everything would be right forever.

Then it vanishes.

The dreamy haze disappears from my mind. The world returns. I sense the soft breeze and gentle chirp of crickets. Turning about, I find myself standing in a clearing. Tall trees loom about, enclosing the area in a make-shift circle. In the center of the space, there stands a statue of a man and a woman.

Both of them wear crowns.

Jacoby steps between me and the stone figures. "What are you doing here?"

"I followed a will-o-the-wisp."

Jacoby frowns. "Or you cast one… and just wish me to *think* you were misled."

I bob my head, angling for a better view of the statues. But each time I shift, Jacoby moves to block my view. "Clearly, you don't want me to look at these two.

You must know that only makes them more interesting."

Jacoby eyes me for a long moment. Next, he raises his hands to chest-height with his palms facing each other. His horns appear, which is something I've only seen happen once before. With a flash, an orb of blue light appears between Jacoby's palms. I've never seen this before, but there's no question what's happening.

Jacoby's about to cast a spell.

"You want to transport me away from here, don't you?"

Jacoby rolls his eyes. "What gave it away?"

"We all have our secrets, as well as a right to keep them." I gently rest my hand on his wrist. "Don't waste your power. I'll leave if you want me to."

Jacoby tilts his head. For a long moment, the orb still hovers between his palms.

At last, Jacoby lowers his arms. "You may look upon the statues."

"What made you change your mind?"

Jacoby narrows his eyes. "I'm curious why you *chose* to come here. Your reaction to the statues may tell me a lot. "

"I already told you. It wasn't a conscious decision."

"We'll see."

Jacoby steps to one side. I move in for a closer look.

These two figures carry the kind of ethereal beauty that is so particular to elves, such as aristocratic bone structure, wide mouths and lean bodies. Taken together, their features remind me of a particular person. Jacoby. No question about it; these are his parents. The inscription reads, *rest in peace.*

"I'm sorry your parents passed away."

"What makes you say that?"

"There's no missing the family resemblance. And the inscription is easy enough to find."

Jacoby folds his arms over his chest. "Anything else?"

"My parents are gone, too."

"How can you be sure?"

I shrug. "I just know things sometimes."

"Like how you found this spot?"

Now I've seen my share of courtroom television shows. On them, the lead prosecutor gets a certain tension in his body when cross-examining a lying witness. That's the precise stance Jacoby carries right now. He so thinks he has me on this one.

"Hey, I might have cast a spell without knowing it. I am an elf, after all."

"And *why* would you want to visit these statues?" Jacoby moves closer. "Are you searching out my weak spots? Planning to destroy me?"

His words shouldn't cut so deeply, but they do.

"It's like this," I reply. "I've been near you for years, but we never really spent time together before. Back at the garden, you looked at me so intensely. I guess it made some part of me curious about you."

Jacoby moves closer. With gentle movements, he wipes the mascara from beneath my eyes. Everywhere he touches me, he leaves a trail of awareness. "You're such a strange one, Agatha."

"All those years growing up..." I swallow past the nervous lump that just lodged in my throat. "Did you ever wonder about me?"

"No, but perhaps I should have."

My eyes widen in shock. One minute, Jacoby accuses me of trying to destroy him. The next thing I know, he's all touchy-feely and sweet. Normally, I have a sassy comeback for any situation. It goes along with spending years of quality time with Marchesa and Ivy.

But right now? I've got nothing.

So I turn away and examine the statues some more. It's a lot easier than trying to figure out Jacoby. "Your parents are beautiful."

"They died twenty years ago."

"How does that work? You're eighteen."

"My parents cast an enchanted cradle. It produced a new son every nine months until my youngest brother,

Zenoch, was born. There are twenty-four of us in all. Or there were. Frey, as you know, is dead."

"An enchanted cradle? I've never heard of that."

"Elves aren't known for their ability to procreate. My parents wanted to keep the throne safe." Jacoby turns to look at the statues again. His profile is so handsome in the moonlight, it almost hurts to look at him.

"Mother and Father left a number of personal journals behind for us children to read. Excellent advice. Although I've never met them, I feel as if my parents are the ones who keep me alive. Although after meeting you, perhaps having a daughter would have been a more effective succession plan."

Before, Jacoby's anger filled in the air around us. Now a gentle silence takes its place. It's as if we're old friends who don't need to speak in order to understand each other. I crave this connection to go deeper.

"The inscription at the statue's base says they died in the Vassal Wars. I've never heard of that."

"At one time, every fiefdom was a vassal either to the Seelie or Unseelie court. When those two went to war, they summoned all their fiefdoms to fight as well. My family was aligned to the Unseelie. When asked, my parents went into battle. Their bodies were never found."

"Do you even know if this is how your parents looked?"

Jacoby narrows his eyes. An icy sense of menace falls between us. "Do *you*?"

What a shock. Jacoby is back to being a dick.

"No. And in case you're wondering, your moods are shifting so quickly, you're giving me whiplash."

When Jacoby next speaks, his voice takes on a gruff edge. "The Faerie Lands are a tangle of alliances and betrayal. To stay alive, I must know whether or not I can trust you. If my attitude shifts, it's because you confuse me, too. The moment I decide that you're one thing, you do something that proves otherwise."

I worry my lower lip with my teeth. This might be a terrible moment to bring up this idea, but then again, a better opportunity may never show up.

"If you want to know the truth about me, then take me to the ruins of the Seelie Palace. It's supposed to hold a magic mirror that strips away all enchantments. That way, we'll both know the truth."

"Or I'll step into an ambush." Jacoby's mouth winds into a knowing smile. "My dear Agatha, now I'll *never* take you to that spot."

"Why not?"

"To manipulate others into doing your bidding, you must learn to be far more subtle. If you'd tried to persuade me to *avoid* the Seelie Palace, then I'd have dragged you there in a heartbeat."

My shoulders slump with a weight of disappointment. Jacoby is right. *I have no idea what I'm doing.*

I shake my head. "I'm not the kind of person who speaks in double truths and hidden lies. Ivy says that I'm an awkward beam of light, shining into places that are best left in shadow."

Jacoby moves even closer. This time, he's near enough that I sense his body heat. The prince sets his knuckle under my chin. Little by little, Jacoby lifts my gaze to meet his. For a long moment, he scans my face.

"I'm not a liar," I declare.

"No fae is. That's why we speak in double-truths."

For a moment, my heart soars. "Does that mean we're going to the Seelie Palace?"

Jacoby chuckles. "I do enjoy learning new games. Do you know what I think yours is? You pretend not to play." He drops his hand. The moment I lose his touch, it's like the temperature drops twenty degrees.

"How very devious of you," adds Jacoby. "But it still won't work. You can forget any hope that I'll take you to the Seelie Palace."

And again, Jacoby goes from one extreme to another. It's enough to make a girl crazy. I set my fists on my hips. "Here's what you don't get about me. I'll find a way to those ruins anyway."

At my words, Jacoby's eyes widen ever so slightly. Somehow, I struck another nerve. I just wish I knew which one. Is he frightened? Intrigued? Angry? The man works the finest poker face ever.

I simply must figure him out. It's my best way to discover that mirror.

PRINCE JACOBY

13

JACOBY

*W*hat is it with this girl?

Agatha is far more intriguing and confusing than I ever thought possible.

I brought her to my private retreat because this place is so well protected with magic, it's the safest spot on Earth or Faerie. And when you have someone like Nal'Adel taking an interest in your future, security is a huge concern. Otherwise, it's not like I have regular visitors to my lands.

As a matter of fact, I've never had anyone here before.

In other words, there are no maps or guides to my property. Yet somehow, Agatha easily found her way into my most secret sanctuary. She acted as if she was just following an errant point of light.

I doubt it.

Turning, I march away from the statues of my parents and march toward my cottage at full speed. Soon, I've left the clearing behind and navigate through a dark maze of trees, hedges and shadows. If Agatha wants a warm place to sleep tonight, she can just keep up.

As I speed along, my thoughts circle back to Agatha once more. That girl must have cast a spell that led to those statues. It's the only way she could have found my parents' memorial. And to think, I'd almost believed her act about being the put-upon stepsister.

She's a secret player.

Still, I find myself wondering if she's finding her way. Checking over my shoulder, I scan the path behind me.

No Agatha.

Bands of worry tighten around my chest. My lands are populated with magical warrior beasts. If Agatha steps onto the wrong path, she could end up at the wrong end of a set of bull horns.

Suddenly, Agatha turns a corner and appears before me. For a long moment, she simply stands in a pool of light. A quiet kind of strength radiates around her.

Agatha tilts her head. "Are we walking together now?"

My answer is immediate. "Yes."

"Good."

"But for your safety only."

Agatha mock-curtsies. "How kind."

We step along, side by side. A pleasant silence hangs between us. Eventually, we step out from the forest and into open territory. Soon we reach a glistening lake surrounded by massive willow trees. It isn't a conscious choice, but we simply stand beside each other and soak in the view.

"What's it called?" asks Agatha.

"Sweet Willow Cove."

"Are the waters safe? It's very elf-like to give something a nice name and then fill it with things that can kill you."

I chuckle. "Yes, it's fine. I've enchanted it to be both warm and free of predators."

The willow trees create a kind of loose wall before us. Countless tiny leaves rustle in the breeze. Suddenly, the long branches part like curtains on a stage. One of my Fortitude herd steps out from the shadows and into the open.

It's Xanthos, my lead bull. He's all raw power on four legs.

I set my hand on Agatha's shoulder. "Don't be afraid."

"I'm not." That's what Agatha says, but the words come out about an octave too high to be believable. I can't help but smile. For someone who gives off such power, it's endearing for her to be frightened by my beastly friends.

"His name is Xanthos." I step over to my bull's side and look toward Agatha. "It's all right. Xanthos won't hurt you."

Little by little, Agatha approaches Xanthos. Once she's close to the animal, Agatha raises her arm. I take her palm in mine and place it on the bull's neck. Her shoulders visibly relax. "So warm." She starts to run her palm down his flank. Xanthos snuffles.

I grin. "That means he likes you."

"I'm glad." Agatha pets Xanthos' flank a few more times before speaking again. "Do you have many Earth animals here?"

"It's an even mix between earth and fae. About two hundred beasts in all. Elves and humans can be rather tricky sometimes. I enjoy the company of my herd."

"I can see why." She leans in closer to Xanthos. "You're a big sweetie, aren't you?"

The bull snuffs out a breath. "Yeah."

Agatha freezes. "Did he just talk to me?"

"Yeah," repeats Xanthos. Hands down, this is his favorite word.

Agatha rounds on me, her eyes wide. "Bulls don't do this on Earth."

"Indeed, Xanthos does originally come from Texas. It took him two months living in the Faerie Lands before he could speak."

"Magic," grunts Xanthos.

"That's right," I say. "Magic changes everything. And rarely for the better, although that's certainly not the case with Xanthos. Magic has transformed him into the self-appointed leader of my extended herd."

Xanthos scrapes at the ground with his front hoof. It's what he always does when there's a big announcement to be made. "Frey," he declares.

"What does that mean?" asks Agatha.

"My late brother, Frey, kept some cows. Xanthos wants to know if I can add them to my herd." I refocus on Xanthos. "How many are there?"

"Fifty," replies Xanthos. "Hurt."

My shoulders slump. "I was afraid of that."

Agatha frowns. "Frey's cattle are injured? How did that happen?"

"Frey," answers Xanthos.

"My late brother was overly attached to his sentient bovines. He lived in the fields with them, which does nothing for an elf's personal hygiene. I'd heard rumors he was preventing them from eating or getting healers." I refocus on Xanthos. "Where's the new herd now?"

"South field."

Rounding on Agatha, I gesture along the trail. "You can follow this path to the cottage. It's set up like a human dwelling. You should be able to find whatever you need."

Agatha lifts her chin. "I'm going with you."

"No, you're not."

Xanthos sniffs. "Power."

There's no question what Xanthos means here. Ever since her energy surge at the castle, there's no missing the aura of magic that surrounds Agatha. If I leave her alone, she could very well wander off my property and find any kind of trouble. My lands are warded to keep fae *out*, not *in*.

I'm wary, and that's *not* because I wanted to kiss Agatha before. This is pure coincidence.

"Xanthos is right," says Agatha. "If your new herd is sick or hungry, I might be able to cast spells that help them."

I tilt my head, as if there were still some actual debate about what to do next. "You may join me, but you must promise to stay out of the way."

"Nice try, Jacoby," she says. "You're not as good at hiding your emotions as you think. Your herd needs power, and now you know I have some." She turns to Xanthos. "Where's the South field?"

In reply, white light surrounds Xanthos. His muscles twist and change. His head and hooves remain, but the rest of him transforms into a man.

A minotaur.

"This way," says Xanthos.

Agatha shoots me the side-eye. "When were you planning to tell me about this?"

I shake my head. "My dear Agatha, I'm still unconvinced you didn't know the truth all along."

"Wow. You've got some serious trust issues."

"It goes along with being an elf, royal, and alive, all at the same time."

With that, we follow Xanthos to check. It's more than a little unsettling. I've never had anyone visit my lands... see the statues of my parents... and now meet my herd. Like it or not, I'm allowing someone I don't trust deeper into my life.

Chances are, this is a massive mistake.

14

JACOBY

*X*anthos takes off at a slow pace. With every step, he leads me and Agatha closer to the South fields. As I march along, my mind fogs over with questions.

Who is this girl, really?

What's my next move?

When we reach the South fields, all thoughts of power and scheming instantly vanish. The cows here are little more than skin and bones. Some even have open wounds. I stroll through the herd, making notes of which animals are in the worst shape. I'll attend to those first.

The first sick animal I find is a pregnant heifer. How this poor thing is still standing, I'll never know.

"I'm Jacoby," I state. "What's your name?"

When the animal speaks, it's between heavy gulps of air. "Daisy."

"Okay, Daisy. I'm here to help you with magic. Do you understand that?"

Her eyes grow wind with panic. "Frey."

Of course, Daisy suspects that I'm here to hurt her. When I next speak, I take care to gentle my voice. "Frey was my brother, but I'm nothing like him."

Agatha steps up to Daisy. "Xanthos led you to these lands, didn't he?"

Daisy's reply is a whisper. "Yes."

"You'll be all right now." Agatha reaches forward. An orb of golden light appears on her outstretched palm. Agatha blows across her hand; her breath sends the orb floating toward Daisy. The moment the sphere of power touches the heifer's hide, the animal changes. Her muscles grow larger. Daisy's skin no longer hangs as loose.

There are two important things about this moment. First is the fact that Agatha definitely wields moon power of some kind. There's no mistaking that particular shade of golden-yellow in that orb—it's the hue of a harvest moon. Second, Agatha was telling the truth. She clearly has no idea how to cast. I must focus and summon my powers. I've never seen someone simply raise their hand and pull up an orb before. Agatha works on instinct.

All my contemplations end when the heifer bellows. "Calf!"

Agatha pales. "What's wrong?"

"It's your spell," I state. "It's made her strong enough to give birth."

From here, there are no long conversations. Agatha and I simply fall into an easy rhythm. I cast spells to heal the baby; Agatha focuses on giving magical strength to Daisy. Power orbs gently float through the air. Hours pass slowly. In the end, we have a healthy calf.

Agatha turns to me and beams. "We did it!"

"Yes, we did." Pain spikes in my heart, but that's just a coincidence. It's not because I've never birthed a calf with someone else before.

"There's more to do," adds Agatha. "Look at this herd!"

It takes me a second to catch my thoughts, but then I point to another animal across the field. "That one needs us next."

And so we go to work again. Once more, Agatha and I settle into an easy rhythm. It's as if we've been working together for years.

It's dark by the time we heal the last of the herd. In the moonlight, I realize that we've had an audience for our efforts. My best Fortitude wait in a neat line. Xanthos marches over.

"They want to meet her," he says.

I stare between my most powerful animals and the small form of Agatha. Like me, they must sense the magic within her. It's only natural for them to be curious.

"Of course." I turn toward Agatha. "Would you like to meet my menagerie?"

Agatha scans the line. There are minotaurs, ice steeds and sentient bears. Even my battle tigers came out to greet her.

"They're all warriors," she says in a hushed voice.

"Correct. If I need them, I transport these members of my herd to Earth for a fight. When I'm here in the Faerie Lands, I train them."

"So you're an elf-warrior-cowboy."

"I'm a prince of the Fortitude. This is our magic."

"Yes, I'd very much like to meet them."

As Agatha steps past each member of my herd, they bow their heads. I'm not sure what hour it is when the review finishes. Eventually, Agatha and I slog back toward my cottage.

The place is as pristine and empty as ever. Somehow, having Agatha here makes the rooms come alive. My guest steps around in a slow circle. "This isn't what I expected. Did you conjure it into existence yourself?"

"I did." I scan the interior, seeing it through Agatha's eyes. "Most elvish decor is more gilded. We Fortitude tend toward the rustic. My brother Frey took it to an extreme, but that's another story."

"I like it."

It shouldn't make me so happy that a random fae approves of my home, yet it does.

"Would you like to see your room?"

"Yes, thank you."

I lead Agatha to my extra bedroom. It's a clean and snug space with fabric-covered walls and an exceedingly fluffy bed.

Agatha plunks onto the mattress. "Oh, this is comfy."

"Glad you approve."

Without further ado, Agatha curls up on her side and instantly falls asleep. I pull off her boots, place a blanket over her and leave her to rest.

As I close the door behind me, an odd sensation takes up residence in my chest. It's as if cords of connection now wind about my heart, linking me to Agatha. When I step away, it pulls on those ties until fresh pain spikes in my heart.

I rub my palm against the ache in my chest. There's no question about it. Agatha is having a strange effect on me. I must either find out her true powers or get rid of her. Soon.

15

JACOBY

*T*hat night, I sleep well. If anything, I get too much rest. It's the only explanation as to why I wake up just after dawn feeling as if an electrical charge were running through my body.

This emotion comes awfully close to excitement. It's as if I can't wait to see Agatha this morning, discuss yesterday's adventures and check on our new herd.

Which is ridiculous.

The only reason I'm alive today is that I make no ties with other fae. Elle is an exception as she's a sweet girl who wields exceptional levels of power.

Yet Agatha's different.

This mystery girl is defiant and, worse, she sees through me in ways that not even Elle managed to do. My herd likes her, which is a risk. I don't need them getting attached to anyone but me. And Agatha has unknown ties to moon magic and possibly Nal'Adel herself.

All of which is why I fight the urge to conjure breakfast for my guest. Agatha can fend for herself. Instead, I head out to Sweet Willow Cove, strip off my robe and wade into the warm waters. It's my regular ritual to swim along the shoreline under the cover of long branches. I'm half-way around the lake when I hear it.

Someone's humming a tune.

My animals are sentient, but they aren't exactly musical. I angle myself for a better view through the willows.

Agatha's here.

She floats on her back while humming away. Like me, she isn't wearing a stitch of clothing.

Now, I shouldn't watch her. That said, my people are aligned to the Unseelie Fae. We're supposed to embody all things dark and sneaky. So it's actually in support of my people's heritage that I fail to announce myself right away. And it turns out, this is one girl who should never wear baggy clothing.

She's beyond lovely.

A moment later, I couldn't say anything if I tried. For the first time, I notice a mark on Agatha's hip.

And it's glowing.

Again, just when I decide that Agatha is one thing, a clue arises that's she's actually another. Some houses mark their elves to show where they fall in the hierarchy. Why is Agatha pretending not to know who she is when it's literally written on her skin?

This girl confuses me to no end.

16

AGATHA

I float on my back and stare at the lightening sky. Dawn is almost here. The moon's image fades to a ghost-like hue. The morning suns close in on the horizon line, sending a bright aura up into what's left of the night sky. The sight is so lovely, I can't help but hum a few bars of *You Are my Sunshine.*

Awareness skitters through my consciousness. Somehow, I know I'm not alone. Flipping in the water, I move to stand on the sandy lake bed. Rings of movement shift out across the still lake. A heady mix of joy and terror battle it out inside me.

"Jacoby? Is that you?"

There's the barest swish of water. Long moments pass before Jacoby himself surfaces about a yard away from me. Water adds a sheen of glossy perfection to the sharp lines of his face. And I've never seen his dark eyes more intent.

Words tumble from my mouth, seemingly on their own. "You're staring."

"It's understandable." He grins. "You're glowing."

On reflex, I set my hand on my throat. "You aren't enough to make me glow."

"No, there's something silver in the water. It appears to be on your hip."

I slap my free hand over my mark. "None of your business," I say quickly.

"Quite right." There's something predatory in his eyes as Jacoby moves closer. "And I'm no concern of yours, either."

Jacoby leans in, stopping when his mouth is just above mine. Our warm breath mingles with the cool lake air. Jacoby closes his eyes. I do the same.

And I wait.

Isn't this when the kissing starts?

I open my eyes to see that Jacoby has lifted his head a little. We're still within kissing range, but now the prince's eyes are open. The intense look remains in his eyes, only there's less heat in his stare.

Jacoby turns and swims off. I watch him leave, feeling as if part of my own soul is being torn away. As

Jacoby steps out of the water, a glimmer of magic shows along his back. Turns out, Jacoby not only has horns.

He also has wings.

I don't know much about royal elf culture, but I'm pretty sure of one thing. It's a big deal to purposely show your true elfy self to someone else... or to lose your grip on your own glamour spell. If it's the former, then Jacoby feels more comfortable around me. But if it's the latter, then I must have upset him somehow.

My insides still feel all tingly from our almost-kiss. I'm used to spending my days trying to avoid being noticed. But getting not only attention, but mixed signals?

That's way beyond me.

17

ELLE

*a*lec and I have been in document hell for almost a week. Still, we finally did it.

We broke the binder code.

Working together, Alec and I organize the mishmash of sheets into a single thing. Turns out, the binder is indeed a contract for the Glass Slipper Ball. The pages list out tons of things that have to happen. As CEO, Alec must approve it all.

From there, we found three areas of sketchy stuff. Those sheets are now divided up into haphazard piles that cover my apartment floor. We found three main places where the proverbial 'red flags' are flying high.

First, something weird is happening at the L Center. This is the Le Charme family's expo hall, so it makes sense they'd hold the ball there. But according to the binder, the company is digging a new *something or other* right below the stage. What's that all about?

Second, the Queen of Hearts isn't being invited to anoint the winners. Which makes sense, considering how she's on an adventure with Colonel Mallory, Alec and Bry. Still, the Queen of Hearts uses her magic to declare the ball's prince and Cinderella. So who's running the show this time?

Third, the docs specifically mention that Elle Cynder is attending the ball in order to find her prince. Guess what? I'm already Alec's girlfriend, so why does anyone think that I would agree to this?

Our list of questions are set.

Tomorrow is the big board meeting.

Alec and I decide to get an early night's sleep. I'm under my covers and about to drift off to dreamland when I see her.

Skye.

Matter of fact, the genie is pretty hard to miss, considering how she's hanging upside down from my ceiling again.

"Howdy," says Skye.

"What do you want?"

"I have a gift for you in honor of tomorrow. It's for good luck."

Now, I've been around enough Magicorum to know

that accepting gifts is a tricky business. I might think I'm getting myself a free lunch, but I could also be agreeing to an eternity in servitude.

Still the offer has me interested. I love me some presents. I sit upright.

"What is it?" I ask.

Skye floats down from the ceiling to set a small item on my comforter. It's a tiny glass lamp. Seeing the small item, I can't help but smile. My parents founded a company called Cynder Mercantile. They employed animates—meaning enchanted objects—who all had artistic skills. One of my favorites was Kokkivo, a phoenix sculpture who made other glass creations.

This lamp is definitely one of Kokkivo's finest pieces of work. There's no missing the swirl of color and light within the glass.

I lift the lamp gingerly from the coverlet and cradle it in my hands. "Where did you get this?"

"What's more important is why I acquired it in the first place. You think genies are unhinged and ugly. But look at this lamp. Some folks think our lore is beautiful."

I set the glass sculpture onto my nightstand. "It's lovely. Thank you."

"Sometimes those who look most unbalanced are that way because we carry a great and invisible load.

Trust me, genies are important. That's why we can't die out."

I stare at the glittering gift. "But you choose to spend eternity trapped inside a lamp."

"No, we're forever free. Getting imprisoned is what happens when you're not careful." A dark gleam shines in her eyes. "Anyone can get imprisoned inside a magical object."

I frown. "Is that a threat?"

"No, it's an opportunity."

"Look, I appreciate your interest, but I don't want to be a genie. I'm already a Cinderella. As a matter of fact, I'm helping my prince with a Glass Slipper Ball, so my template is stronger than ever. This genie thing isn't going to happen with me. You need to adjust and move on."

"So you say." Skye pulls her Stetson low over her eyes. White smoke surrounds her in a cloud of power. The haze swirls for a moment before dissipating. Then all the haze vanishes. Skye is gone as well.

I should be relieved, yet for some reason, I want to call her back. Life is weird.

Shaking it off, I scooch back under my covers and try to fall asleep. It takes hours, but I eventually nod off. In my dreams, I fly over the Faerie Lands. The rolling green hills undulate beneath me. It's beyond beautiful. I look back to check out my wings.

Only they aren't there.

And neither are my legs.

I'm a genie.

18

ALEC

6:08 AM

I pace in the empty boardroom of the Le Charme Building. As of this moment, it's just me, the grandfather clock and an empty table. Lifting my phone, I recheck the text from Elle.

CallMeElle: Can u meet @6? Le Charme board rm

MagicMan: Sure. C U there

Now Elle is only nine minutes late, but she's also been stalked by enchanted humans. I'm not the kind of warlock who waits around and assumes that the love of his life is fine. I type a quick reply.

MagicMan: U ok

I hit *send* and wait. Sadly, the screen comes back with a big red exclamation mark of failure. It's easy to see why. There's no signal in this building. Part of me wants to chuck my phone out the window. After all, this is one of the many reasons why I wanted to fix the contract with WorldWeb before signing. We have total crap for internet and phone.

I check the clock again. Elle is now ten minutes late. I decide to give her until 7:15 AM. After that? I'm casting some major spells.

As I always do in the board room, I strip off my sport coat, set it onto the back of my chair and try to get comfortable. It isn't easy.

Elle, please be safe.

The main door swings open. I exhale. *At last, Elle has arrived.* My heart lightens at the prospect of seeing her again.

Only it's not Elle who walks through the door.

Instead of my girlfriend, it's my parents who march into the room. Like always, they could be the cover models for a magazine called Rich White People Who Hate You. At the sight of this pair, my stomach tumbles while my brain freezes. I've spent hours preparing for a very different morning. How did my parents get loose?

Right now, that doesn't matter. If Legend and Diamond are here, it's not a good thing.

A realization appears. My parents must have been hiding in the outer hallway, waiting for me to do what I always do when I enter this stuffy board room—set my sport coat onto the back of my chair. Once that was done, they swept into the chamber.

There can only one reason why.

Once my jacket is out of reach, so are all my magical gemstones.

Turning, I lunge for my sport coat. But Legend is too fast for me. He already has a magical rock of his own that grasped in his fist. White light bursts from between his fingers. One moment, my jacket sits on the back of a chair. The next, it's gripped in Legend's hand.

My mind races through scenarios. I could try to run, but my parents are blocking the door. I've no gemstones to use and fight them. Also, my phone is dead. Which leaves one final option. I can try to talk myself out of this.

"So what do we do now?" I ask.

Legend grins. "Why, chat with your chairman, of course."

The Duke enters the room. A copy of the infamous black binder is cradled in his arms. He sets the item onto the tabletop with a thunk.

"I brought another one for you to sign." The Duke pats the binder like it's a kitten. "Everything about the Glass Slipper Ball is in here." He pulls another quill pen from the folds of his suit coat and sets it beside the binder. "With your parents around to explain, I'm sure you'll sign this right away."

In this moment, two facts become clear. First, it's a good thing Elle hasn't arrived. There are some parts of my messy life that she just doesn't need to see. Second, there is *no way* I'm signing that pile of trash.

When I next speak, my voice carries the edge of frustration. "I still have questions, *chairman*."

"And your parents will answer them all," counters the Duke. "Please don't take this as a personal betrayal. It's only business." The Duke stares at me with his milky eyes. I think he's actually waiting for me to forgive him.

Let's just say I'm not in the mood.

"Pack up your desk," I declare. "You're out of here."

The Duke gives me an indulgent smile. "How quaint." He turns to my parents. "Thank you for coming here and explaining things to the boy. I know you'll get that binder signed today." The Duke lumbers off, careful to close the door behind him.

My parents step deeper into the chamber. Up close, I can see they haven't changed a bit. Legend is all blond hair, blue eyes, and irresistible charm. Diamond has even features, long brown hair and a dancer's grace.

Seeing them again sends waves of revulsion moving through me. How many hours did I spend floating in magical space while their spells tried to brainwash me?

Far too long.

And now they're free.

The air becomes charged with power. Darkness creeps into the corners of the room. Outside the wall of windows, shadows slide over the city. Ever so subtly, the sun transforms into a yellow harvest moon. This is something humans won't be able to detect. But as a member of the Magicorum, I can't miss it.

It all adds up to one conclusion. My parents didn't escape the Faerie Lands without help. And there's only one elf who wields magic that stems from both darkness and the moon. Nal'Adel. Is she the one who's behind my parents' escape?

One way to find out.

"Nal'Adel should never have set you two loose," I declare. Then I wait for their reaction.

Legend's eyes widen slightly. He hides his surprise quickly enough, but I still caught his look of shock.

"That's not true," says Legend. "We don't even know any Nal'Adel."

"Don't bother lying," I counter. "Your expression just confirmed everything."

"Fine," says Diamond. "Nal'Adel did help us."

"How do you know so much about elves?" asks Legend. "You must have your allies in the Faerie Lands."

"As a matter of fact, I do." I fold my arms over my chest. "You know one of them very well. *Colonel Mallory the Magnificent.* He won't be happy that Nal'Adel set you free. The Colonel is super protective of Elle, and by extension, he looks out for my welfare too."

Legend chuckles. "Then it's such a shame that the Colonel is off on a wild goose chase. You and Elle are totally alone here, son. There will be no help coming to you, whether it's from the Colonel, Knox or Bryar Rose. Even the Queen of Hearts is out of range."

My thoughts wheel through this news. A single fact becomes clear. "Nal'Adel lured our friends off onto this mysterious quest, didn't she? She wants to remove anyone who could help me and Elle."

"Quite right," confirms Diamond. "Nal'Adel is an excellent planner. She sets schemes with schemes."

A realization slams into me. "Elle didn't text me this morning."

"I'm afraid not," says Legend with mock-sadness. "That was all my idea. I control your phone with a special app built for me by WorldWeb."

Anger heats my blood. I glance at my phone on the conference room table. With every corner of my being, I want to grab the thing and chuck it at Legend's face. Still, I keep my temper in check.

It's time to focus on *why* this is happening. The binder on the tabletop is the big giveaway.

"This is all about the Glass Slipper Ball," I declare. "Nal'Adel wants Elle there. Why?"

My parents share a long and meaningful look. It's Diamond who breaks the silence. "I'm sure we don't know."

What a lie.

The wheels of my mind spin even faster. I'm the warden of witch and wizard magic. Elle is the warden for fae power. That's why the Colonel took her wings when she was a baby—it was all to hide Elle away from those who would try to steal her magic. Now it's my parents who are helping those who wish to hurt Elle. Protective energy streams through my limbs. A single thought echoes through my soul.

Defend Elle.

"Listen to me," I demand. "Nal'Adel is wrong about Elle having tons of power. Much of Elle's magic was recently released through the pyramids. If the Colonel hadn't gotten tricked into leaving, he could explain everything right now."

Legend chuckles. "You mean Elle's powers as a warden?"

It takes everything in me not to stagger backward. "You know about that?"

"I must admit," says Legend. "The tracker that WorldWeb put on your phone is rather shoddy. Even so, it was enough for me to figure out what Elle truly was, and that's a warden of magic. Sadly, I also know she recently lost the best of her powers. And I certainly told Nal'Adel all about that. But Nal'Adel is convinced that your Elle is filled with some important stuff."

"It's not our place to correct an elf," adds Diamond.

Once more, my parents share another long look. The best way to describe the expression between them is with one word: *smug*.

Facts about Nal'Adel spin through my mind. The Faerie Lands are made of hundreds of fiefdoms. All these little realms consider themselves to be King and Queen of something or other. In each fiefdom, the powers some in pairs.

It doesn't take long to figure out what the Mistress of Moonshadow would want with Elle. "Nal'Adel's fiefdom doesn't have an opposite."

"That's not true!" exclaims Diamond.

"It's public knowledge," I counter. "Just surf Magic Web. Everyone knows that Nal'Adel is the Mistress of

Moonshadow, but she doesn't have a Mistress of Moonbeams to balance her out. Nal'Adel is less powerful without an opposite." I rub my neck as I think things through. "Nal'Adel must think Elle has the power of the Mistress of Moonbeams."

A charged silence fills the room.

That's as good as my parents saying: *yes, Nal'Adel, the Mistress of Moonshadow, thinks that Elle is her Mistress of Moonbeams.*

My eyes widen. "The Glass Slipper Ball has nothing to do with boosting sales for Le Charme. Nal'Adel is making you hold it in order to lure in Elle. Jacoby is the bait. And the stalker humans are extra inspiration, all to get Elle to attend. Then, once Elle's there, Nal'Adel will magically drain her."

Legend chuckles. "Every so often, I see a little bit of my natural brilliance in you. Yes, Nal'Adel wants to take Elle's magic. It's a very tricky spell and must be done both on Earth and in the Faerie Lands. Indeed, that's the whole reason for the Glass Slipper Ball."

"It's so silly," adds Diamond. "Elle simply can't be the Mistress of Moonbeams. But Nal'Adel insists that's the truth. Elle carries some kind of magical signature, blah blah blah. And since the Mistress of Moonbeams promised to set us loose, we agreed to help her, no matter how stupid it all sounds."

Legend shoots an angry look at Diamond. "Hush!"

I scan the darkened room with new eyes. "She's in this room, isn't she?"

My parents don't reply. Again, that's essentially a confirmation of the truth.

When I next speak, I take care to raise my voice. "Why don't you step forward, Nal'Adel?"

Long seconds tick by before a figure materializes from the shadows. Even before I see her face, I know the truth.

Nal'Adel is here.

NAL'ADEL

19

ALEC

Outside of Jacoby, I haven't met any elf royalty before. Nal'Adel wears an elaborate red gown with an armored breastplate. Her skin is almost pure white, as are the loops of hair atop her head. Both her ears and eyebrows are so pointed and long, they remind me of antennae.

Yet that's not the most elf-like thing about her. Nal'Adel stares at me in a way that suggests I'm prey. Typical.

Nal'Adel inhales deeply. "Elle's stench is on you. It's so faint, yet I still scent the power of moonbeams."

I tilt my head, confused. I spent hours with Elle last night. Why would the scent of her power be faint?

Well, whatever the reason, it doesn't change the big

danger here. Nal'Adel is targeting Elle. That needs to end, now.

"Leave Elle alone," I declare.

"Why should I?" asks Nal'Adel. "Can't you see what a great chance this is? Look at your friend Jacoby. His fiefdom wields the power of Fortitude and is offset by the realm of Miniscule. Both sides want to drain the other, yet the most they can do is sip a little power when the other isn't looking. But Elle? She brims with magic and has no idea how to protect herself. I can drain her and become the greatest force in all the Faerie Lands. Who wouldn't want that?"

I scan her carefully. Nal'Adel is clearly clever. Then again, all living elf royalty must be smart to survive. So why is she babbling all her strategy to me?

"You need me to sign that contract, don't you?"

Nal'Adel arches her brows. "The Le Charme company is tied to a set of ancient spells. Once you became CEO, that magic demands you must approve certain changes."

My eyes widen. "That's why you're making changes to the stage at the L Center. You must connect the worlds of Faerie and Earth in order to enact your draining spell."

"Quite right." Nal'Adel looks to Legend. "You misspoke before. This boy is smarter than either of you."

I sort through everything I know of draining spells. "My parents are correct about one thing: Elle is not the Mistress of Moonbeams. Whatever spell you cast on her won't drain anything of value. You'll only end up killing her."

Nal'Adel shrugs. "And why would I care about that?"

I step closer. "Because you're here to persuade me to sign that binder. Let me guess. Next you'll offer what I most want in the world. Maybe you even think it will be power or my freedom, just as it was with my parents."

"Clever again," says Nal'Adel. "But it was your parents who were supposed to get you to sign that binder. I'm here with another offer. Tie yourself to me magically. Then I can approve anything without ever consulting you again. I give you two choices. One, you may join my men's harem as a lower-level husband. Two, I imprison you for eternity in a way that makes you part of me."

To emphasize her point, Nal'Adel taps the jeweled necklace around her throat. As a wizard, I know a lot about gemstones. That one is packed with power and could be used as a magical dungeon.

"What do you say?" asks Nal'Adel.

"I choose the prison."

Nal'Adel chuckles. "You can't be serious."

"You're asking me to marry you. That's something

which can never be undone and my heart belongs to someone else. So go ahead and lock me up because I know one thing. Elle will find me and set me loose. Then together, we'll take you down."

"If prison is what you want, then I will place you there."

"You promised to marry Alec," says Diamond. "You gave your word!"

Nal'Adel waves her hand dismissively. "That's worth nothing. If you want anything from a fae, you ask for a binding vow."

Diamond lifts her chin. "You're the truly stupid one. Here you go, making all this fuss for a little slut with barely any magic."

A long pause follows. A heavy air of anticipation fills the room. Everyone knows that Mother has said too much, with the possible exception of Diamond herself.

"I don't like you," states Nal'Adel. She snaps her fingers. Cords of shadow whip out from the corners of the room. Moving in unison, they stab Diamond through at a dozen places at once.

My mother falls over, dead.

Sadness presses in around me. Between my two parents, I was far closer to Diamond. And whatever her faults, Diamond didn't deserve to die.

"Such a shame," announces Nal'Adel. "Now only two

men remain to entertain me. Who should I destroy next?"

Legend crumples to his knees. "I'm your loyal ally. Please don't hurt me."

Nal'Adel turns to me. "Looks like you've been betrayed again. And what do you say to that?"

I lean against the wall, hitching my right ankle over my left. "I say that as much as you enjoy toying with prey, it doesn't impress me. I won't fall down like Legend."

"We'll see." Raising her arms, Nal'Adel sends a wave of power that slams into me. Pain zings through every nerve ending in my body. I sense myself twisting and folding as I enter an eternal and darkened space.

As my world fades to nothingness, I cling to a final thought.

I will see Elle again.

ELLE

6:42AM
I've tried out ten outfits for this morning's board meeting. With the help of my favorite stuffed animal, I think I finally nailed the look.

"What do you think, Mister Moose?" As my fave, my little white moose is angled to look into the mirror with me.

Twisting from side to side, I check myself out. I wear the same black cocktail dress Alec picked out before, only I've paired it with a big hat. My long hair is braided and totally stylish. I also wear a little bit of make-up and a lot of sass. Bubble gum helps, too. These old guys won't know what hit them.

"I agree," I tell my stuffed moose. "This look is the bomb."

All in all, I look mighty professional, if I do say so myself. Totally ready to take on the board of directors for Le Charme.

Alec insisted on transporting me to the Le Charme Building, but he isn't supposed to arrive for a few minutes yet. I have just enough time to check on my stalker situation.

Crossing my bedroom, I look out my window and scan the sidewalk below.

My enchanted humans hold all new signs today. The words make my legs turn wobbly beneath me. All the placards say the same thing.

Rest in Peace, Alec

An electric wave of terror pulses through me.

No, no, no.

Rushing over to my bed, I flip open my laptop. A news announcer with slicked-back hair fills the screen.

"And now," he states. "We'll go to a live stream."

The camera switches to a view of the L Center stage. The place is all busted up. Piles of wood are stacked all around.

So far, that's expected.

Alec's binder said the company is doing some strange construction on the L Center. What's shocking is who stands on the only stable part of that stage.

Legend le Charme.

I never expected Alec's father to stay in the Faerie Lands forever, especially with someone like Nal'Adel as a possible ally. Still, Legend and Diamond have only been gone six weeks. That seems a little fast to escape.

On my small screen, Legend begins to speak. "My heartfelt thanks to the members of the press who are here today. I truly appreciate you coming by on such short notice."

Legend pauses as flashbulbs go off. He turns from side to side, probably giving the reporters different angles for their shots.

Wow. Do I ever hate this guy.

Legend continues. "I have such sad news. My son Alec has just died unexpectedly. He tried to cast a spell beyond his skill and..." Here Legend takes in a long and dramatic breath. "It ended his life. What a tragedy. The loss has been so shocking that my dear wife, Diamond, has checked herself into a private care facility for the foreseeable future."

The world around me takes on a dream-like sheen. *Alec is dead? That can't be right.*

Legend is a lying liar. *I'll find Alec on my own, thank*

you very much. Closing my eyes, I summon up my magic and picture Alec.

"Take me to him," I whisper.

This time the power is right where I need it. Pink fairy dust whirls around me, faster and faster. When the magic stops, I'm still in my apartment.

No Alec.

No news.

Oh, no.

Legend keeps talking to reporters. "Alec's body has already been cremated and released to the wind. He's part of magic now."

Clearly, my magic couldn't find Alec. Is it because my boyfriend has been tossed into the air... or is it because my own casting skills are too weak to finish the spell?

Closing my eyes, I try to summon Bry, Knox and the Colonel. It isn't until my third try that something happens. The fairy dust hovers in the air while taking the form of the Colonel's face.

"Thank you for reaching out to me magically," says the Colonel. "I'm on a bit of an adventure with some friends and will stay out of touch for a while. Please try back again in a month or two."

All of a sudden, it's like I can't pull in enough breath. Alec is dead and I can't speak to my virtual family for months?

Legend continues. "Recently, Diamond and I were supposedly exiled. In truth, we went on an extended world tour. We wanted to give Alec a chance to spread his wings and run the company. We never could have thought..."

My mouth thins to an angry line. *What a bunch of lies.* Legend and Diamond weren't sent on a world tour. Alec's parents were sent into exile. Everyone knows that, don't they?

Yet the reporters don't even raise so much as a question. I check the chat stream beside the video on my laptop. Everyone's asking which countries Legend and Diamond visited. Someone says they were spotted in Greece.

My heart sinks. It's as if the exile to the Faerie Lands never happened. I'd think this is another spell from Nal'Adel, but I doubt it. Humans believe what they want to believe. And no one can imagine that any parents would be as cruel as Alec's were. Must be nice.

Legend allows yet another dramatic pause to follow before going on. "Alec was only CEO of Le Charme for a short time, but he had a big dream for our company. That's why I wanted to tell you about his passing while standing here, at the L Center. It was Alec's dying wish that we share his secret project."

My mind blanks with shock. Alec's project? What is Legend talking about?

Legend spreads his arms wide. "We're to hold a new Glass Slipper Ball, only this time it will be for an elf prince named Jacoby." He pats under his eyes. "No one can replace our boy, but perhaps together, we can finish the ball the way he wanted it to happen."

Frustration boils through me. Legend and Diamond tortured Alec, trying to brainwash him into being their own little puppet. Alec fought back. He's strong. I don't believe for one second that Alec miscast a spell and ended his own life. If anything, Diamond and Legend somehow took Alec down for their own purposes.

Legend comes back. "I have a final piece of good news. Elle Cynder has promised to attend the new Glass Slipper Ball. It's a fitting tribute to our son's life. Thank you, everyone."

The announcer comes back on soon "That's the end of the impromptu press conference. For those of you who are just joining us, Legend Le Charme has just announced that Elle Cynder—"

That's when I lose it. Grabbing my laptop, I smash it against the wall. Soon the device is nothing but trash.

How dare they?

My phone lets off a beep. My heart lightens, thinking

that maybe Bry is reaching out at last, I pick up my device to find a new email. It's from Legend.

Dear Elle,

By now, you've probably heard the news about Alec's passing. Please know we want you to attend the Glass Slipper Ball. In fact, we insist you go. It's what Alec would have wanted.

Sparkles and love,

Legend

I fight back the urge to crush my phone with a hammer. Rage churns through me as I focus on my enemy.

Nal'Adel.

This is all her doing. For whatever reason, the Mistress of Moonbeams wants me to go to this Glass Slipper Ball. And she's gotten Diamond and Legend to help her reach this goal, all while taking down Alec. Even worse, my step-family is probably in on this, too. Marchesa and Ivy would jump at the chance to take me down.

Even Agatha might help.

I picture my step-sister with her running mascara and baggy dress. She's never been anything but quiet before, but you never know.

Sometimes it's the silent ones that you must fear the most.

JACOBY

*A*fter returning from my ill-fated swim, I change and step into my feasting chamber. By now, I've taken care to dress in my royal best, meaning a long black coat and leather pants. The room looks as it always does, what with its rustic wooden table and garden murals on the walls. Wide windows let in the sunshine.

It's the perfect place to set my trap for Agatha.

I can't believe I was so careless back at Sweet Willow Cove. I don't show my wings to anyone. I must resolve the question of her honesty, once and for all.

I tap into my inner energy, focusing my power between my palms. An orb of magic appears. Waving my arm, I send it out across the table. The sphere bursts and pulls in my favorite delicacies from Earth. There are croissants and fresh fruit, sweet cakes and hot tea. Somewhere on Earth, a bunch of restaurants are now wondering where their orders went.

Could be worse. Many royal houses steal away the best human chefs, forcing them to serve the Faerie Lands. I only do so to their finest meals.

With the food in place, I take my seat at the head of the table and wait for Agatha to enter. Soon enough, she steps inside. Agatha has changed her clothes as well. She now wears a long green gown instead of that baggy mourning dress. The girl has never looked more ethereal or lovely.

I shake my head. There's no point in wasting time mooning over Agatha. The girl is a mystery. For all I know, I could be harboring an assassin in my midst. I need answers.

Agatha steps into the room and pauses. She narrows her eyes. "I can't decide."

"What to eat?"

"No. Whether this is an ambush or a friendly meal."

"Ambush." I grin and gesture to the seat beside me. "Have a seat."

Agatha slides onto her chair. "Before you do *whatever it is you're planning*, there's another thing we need to discuss."

"Go on."

"We need to warn Elle about Nal'Adel."

"Don't worry. I've sent her a message."

"Who? Elle or Nal'Adel?"

"Why, Elle obviously." I can't help but smirk. "But it's impressive that you're starting to think like an elf. One must always look for dual meanings."

"Is that why I'm here? A lesson in lying?"

"In a way." I pour myself a cup of tea. "I'm still not sure if you need lessons... or if you could give them. I'd like to ask you about certain things."

Agatha scoops up a croissant and sets it on her plate. "Will my answers stop you from going hot and cold?"

"With any luck."

"Then please. Ask away."

I've had all morning to rack up my list of questions for this moment. I launch right into my interrogation. "Yesterday when you cast a spell on Daisy, your magic held the color of the moon. Why?"

"I don't know." Agatha fidgets in her chair and sets her hand on her hip.

"Your mark. Does it have to do with the moon?"

Agatha lifts her chin. "That's none of your business."

"Many fiefdoms mark their people. That symbol could tell us both who you are. Show it to me and I'll let you know."

Agatha's face flushes a pretty color of pink. "It's a

moon and three stars. And that's as close to my mark as you'll ever get again."

"Sadly, that doesn't provide any useful information at all. Next question. Do you know my brother, King Gorgan?"

"No."

"What about Mandrake?"

"Who?"

"Every fiefdom has an opposite, like spring and winter or Seelie and Unseelie. For the Fortitude, our magic flows through creatures that are large and powerful. Kaiser Mandrake runs the Miniscule. His abilities are focused on strength that is small and deadly."

Agatha's eyes widen. "You're talking about germs."

"Yes, that's the power he wields. Mandrake wears dark coat and a plague mask. Hard to forget."

"I've never met him."

Just thinking of Mandrake, I can feel a pull on my magic. We enhance each other, but it's not a happy alliance. As with all things in the Faerie Lands, one must be wary of betrayal.

"Are you certain?" I press. "In terms of threats, he's the worst."

"Plague masks are those long and pointed things that look like you're wearing an evil bird costume?"

"Precisely. Have you met him?"

"Never. And I'd remember the plague mask." She pops a blueberry into her mouth. "What else? If this is an interrogation, you better get it all out."

"You tried to kill Elle Cynder."

"Marchesa and Ivy did the evil stuff. I actually helped Elle escape when Marchesa imprisoned her."

I lean forward. "How so?"

"I'd never cast anything that big before. I wanted to help Elle and things just happened."

"Because you can't control your power."

"You saw how it worked with Daisy. I feel things and the power goes to work. That's how it went down with Elle, too."

"And you never told Elle that you're really an elf?"

"No. The best way to keep a secret is to never tell a soul." She sighs. "You don't know what it's like with Marchesa and Ivy. If they ever found out I was an elf, my best scenario would have been getting tossed out on the street."

Much as it is silly to do so, my heart aches for her. "And the worst?"

"Death. If Marchesa knew I had fae magic, she'd try to sell me to someone like the Denarii League so my powers could get harvested."

"Denarii? I thought they were gone."

"According to rumors, a few of them are still running

around. And other groups do the same thing. There's always a black market for stolen magic."

So far, Agatha's story seems consistent. But there are still many threads that hang far too loose for my liking. "When you helped out Elle, do you think you left a magical residue behind?"

"Why do you ask?"

"Nal'Adel is the Mistress of Moonshadow. Her pairing is the Mistress of Moonbeams. But that other Mistress has never appeared. Nal'Adel thinks it's Elle."

"So there's a missing Mistress?"

"Call her a Queen, if you prefer. My brother runs a fiefdom and he certainly names himself as a King."

Agatha bobs her head, considering. "It's possible I left some kind of residue. Like I told you, I don't know how my powers work."

"If you're leaving magical leftovers behind, then your abilities are rather sloppy." I eye Agatha carefully. *Could she be the missing queen?*

Agatha shakes her pointer finger. "No, no, no. I can see where your elfy mind is going with this."

"*You've* an elfy mind as well. It seems to be visiting the same place."

"Don't get any wild ideas. I am not the Mistress of Moonbeams."

"I disagree. If that is your identity, then it would

explain many things. It was right after the Glass Slipper Ball that Nal'Adel's agents decided Elle was the Mistress of Moonbeams. The timing works out. You could have mistakenly placed your power signature on Elle."

Agatha shakes her head. "I don't know who I am, but I'm not this missing queen."

I drum my fingers on the tabletop. A single question reverberates through my mind. *Is Agatha playing at not knowing her identity... or is her confusion real?*

"One last question," I state. "What did you know about this new Glass Slipper Ball?"

"Marchesa and Ivy had been sneaking off to see Nal'Adel for weeks. I found out about it when I first met Lady Cloake. Whatever that Glass Slipper Ball may be, I've had nothing to do with it. I'm not part of my family like you think."

"And yet you allowed yourself to be dragged off into exile with them."

"I thought you were done with questions."

"I lied."

"I allowed myself to go into exile with Ivy and Marchesa, but only to find out who I am and where I belong. I had no idea what Marchesa and Ivy were up to." She sighs. "You think I'm just like the rest of them, don't you?"

"Sometimes."

This is going nowhere. I pull on my inner magic and summon a fresh orb of power. The sphere hovers over the breakfast table.

Agatha sucks in a shaky breath. "What are you doing?"

"I've come to a decision. Or to be accurate, I've had a change of heart. We're going to the Seelie Ruins."

Agatha pales. "But you said you'd never take me. Are you toying with me?"

"In a way," I reply. "You're about to take a look into the Moonbeam Mirror, just as you *claimed* you always wanted." I fix her with a pointed stare. "It seems we both wish to know who you really are."

I send my magical orb into the wall. The blue light spreads across the mural, creating a new wooden door. Rising, I cross the room and pull the handle, revealing a darkened space beyond the threshold.

"Shall we?"

Agatha grins. "Yes. Let's go."

22

AGATHA

*T*he door opens to a gray landscape that spreads under a charcoal-colored sky. I soak in every aspect of this moment.

The rolling mist.

My speeding pulse.

The scent of old stone and new possibilities that wafts in through the opened door.

At last. I'm about to visit the Seelie Palace and see the Moonbeam Mirror. Joy and terror battle it out inside me. It's a crush of emotion that drives a flood of memories through my mind.

My first recollection takes me back to Manhattan.

I stand on Second Avenue. A breeze whips down the sidewalk. A buzzing sensation erupts in my chest. My magic is awake. Frightened, I clutch my floppy hat so tightly over my head, I pop a seam on the brim. I speak the same words over and over, careful to keep my voice to a hush.

"Please don't let my ears show."

Next I recall the place I've spent the last five years of my life. Cynder Mercantile.

I hear their voices before I see them. Elle and Jacoby are talking. I tiptoe through the warehouse until I reach the entrance to the front store. I peep through a small round window that's set into the access door.

A familiar sight greets me through the glass pane. The store itself is a cramped space whose walls were lined with shelves and artsy goods. Elle and Jacoby stand in a corner, their heads close as they whisper secrets.

What would I do if Jacoby wanted to share a secret with me? Would we lean in close, just like he does with Elle?

Suddenly, both Elle and Jacoby burst out into laughter. That's when it happens. The pair notice me. Panic zings down my spine. What do I do? How should I act?

I can't manage a smile, but I do wave in their direction. The movement is mechanical and odd, but it's better than nothing. Elle waves back. Jacoby stares through me as if I don't exist. It hurts far more than it should.

At this point, I realize I've been standing and staring at the doorway for quite a while. Jacoby inspects me closely, his features unreadable.

"Ready?" he asks.

"Yes. Let's go."

I step across the threshold and onto the misty land-scape beyond. It's late morning now, although you wouldn't know it from the sky. The heavens are as grey as the cloud-covered ground. Every so often, a pile of rubble juts up from the mist.

Jacoby lifts his hands. Seconds later, a fresh orb appears between his palms. He turns to me. "The Seelie Palace got razed during the Vassal Wars. The upper grounds are nothing but pitted earth and bog monsters. My orb will lead us onto the right paths for the lower levels. I've heard the palace is still intact down there. If so, that's where we'll find the Moon-beam Mirror."

"Lower levels, got it." In all truth, my adrenaline is spiking so hard at this point, I'm not sure I'll retain half of what Jacoby just said.

"Stay close to the orb. You go first; I'll be right behind in case anything goes wrong."

I arch my right brow. "So you can run away?"

He chuckles. "Now there's the sassy Agatha I know so well. I was starting to worry that you'd lost your nerve."

The orb starts to move. I step along behind it. The landscape is a labyrinth of billowing mist and shattered stone. Even with the orb as a guide, I make a few missteps. Jacoby is always right behind me, his gentle touch at my back when I need it.

The sensation is so nice, I almost forget that we're here because he can't trust me.

Eventually, the orb leads us down a series of stone staircases that loop into the ground. It must have been a massive palace for the place to have so many subterranean levels.

At last, we reach a tall wooden door. The orb pauses by the heavy iron handle.

Jacoby steps up to my side. "Allow me."

"Is it safe?"

"Since the orb hovers by the handle, then that means it's safe enough." He pulls on the handle. The door slowly swings open.

After so much mist and ruined stone, the sight that next greets me is a shock. The chamber within seems untouched. It's a circular space covered in intricately carved stone. As we step inside, candles flare to light, showing off the only item in the room.

A freestanding mirror.

All of a sudden, it's an effort to pull in enough breath. I cross the room to stand before the very object I've waited years to see.

Then I wait before the Moonbeam Mirror.

Minutes pass.

Nothing happens except for how I can watch my own reflection. All I see is the same old Agatha with my melting mascara and lifeless black hair.

Jacoby gently rests his hand on my shoulder. "The Faerie Lands are filled with stories of all kinds of magical things. Some of them simply aren't true."

My stomach sinks. For years, I've wanted this moment. I'm at the Moonbeam Mirror.

And nothing is happening.

I nod, not trusting my voice. Maybe there is no magical way to find out who I am. Or even to prove the truth of my words to Jacoby.

I turn away, ready to leave.

That when the mirror flares to life. Blue lights swirl across the reflective surface. I shift my stance. Once again, I wait before the Moonbeam Mirror. Only this time, a single word escapes my lips.

"Yes."

MOONBEAM MIRROR

23

AGATHA

The moment still doesn't seem real. After so many years of hoping and waiting, I'm watching the Moonbeam Mirror come alive with magic.

The azure light transforms into an image. Although the picture is all in shades of blue, it's clear that it shows a handsome man with long dark hair, high cheekbones and a strong jawline. There's no missing how he has the distinctive ears of an elf. In terms of clothes, he wears a simple velvet robe while a thin ringlet encircles his head. It's a crown.

Behind him, I see the same chamber that I stand in today, only this one is a mess of elves racing about, some with satchels on their backs. Others wear full body armor and march along in neat rows. Somehow, I know that I'm looking into the past. Even better, I know what time I'm viewing as well.

This is the end of the Vassal Wars. Somehow, it's been captured within this mirror.

I look to Jacoby. "What kind of spell is this?"

Jacoby nods toward the mirror. "A shard of that man's soul has been stored in this mirror. All these years, it's stayed trapped in order to talk to you now. That's advanced magic and a great honor."

In the mirror, the man speaks. "Quite right, Prince Jacoby of the Fortitude." He looks to me. "Greetings, I am Wyrran Aire Donnak Elric Luvon, King of Moonbeams."

"Oh." My mouth starts going on its own. "I'm Agatha."

"No," says Wyrran. "Your name is Kir. And if you're seeing me in this mirror, then you're in the Seelie Palace and eighteen years of age." He sighs. "It's time for my work to wane."

I gasp. "You're the one who hid my true nature."

"I cast an obfuscation spell on you." A man and woman race behind Wyrran. In their rush, their sack strikes the king in the shoulder. Wyrran rubs the spot. "In my time, the Vassal Wars are ending. Both sides are about to destroy each other. Seelie and Unseelie plan to launch volleys of attack magic at each other. Their powers don't mix, so they'll only end up creating an even bigger disaster. There will be no winner."

I pull my brows together in confusion. "How can they do that if they know they'll just kill each other?"

"Each side thinks it's strong enough to withstand the other."

"But what about you?" I ask. "Can't you run away?"

There's no missing the genuine look of sorrow in his eyes. "I gave my word. I heed my vows. But I'm doing what I can to save what's left of our people. That's where you enter this story."

My heart seems to leap into my throat. *This is it. The moment.* "Tell me."

"As the war drags on, most of our people have become refugees. One by one, they're being captured by rival fiefdoms and drained for their power. In order to save some of our people, I've found them new places to live on earth. to hide their power, I cast obfuscation spells that would conceal their true identit—"

The mirror hazes over with the same pool of blue that appeared when I first approached it.

"Wyrran?" I turn to Jacoby. "What's going on? Where is the message?"

"The spell is fading," explains Jacoby. "Whatever Wyrran has to tell you, he doesn't have much longer."

Long seconds tick by. My pulse speeds. At last,

Wyrran's face reappears on the mirror. "Know this. Whatever happens, you cannot trust Nal'Adel..." The swirl of blue overtakes the mirror once more.

I look to Jacoby. "Is there anything we can do to boost the spell?"

Jacoby shakes his head. "Wyrran is Seelie; I'm Unseelie. Our magic won't mix. If I try to help his casting, I'll only destroy it. And until you have more control of your powers, you shouldn't try to assist the spell, either."

It's a reflex to move closer to Jacoby and grip his upper arm. I stare into the churning azure on the mirror and hope.

Finally, Wyrran reappears. "I wanted to do the right thing, but I'm afraid I made a mess of things, pumpkin. You're Seelie. Never forget that. Our house is aligned to the right as we see it."

At these words, Jacoby rolls his eyes. No question why, either. Jacoby thinks that the goody-goody Seelie do far more damage than the clearly sketchy Unseelie.

Wyrran keeps speaking, but his words and image keep fading in and out. "There's a future for you, but you must follow... last of the Moonbeam elves... beware the battle.... Kir."

Snap!

The blue mirror shatters into a spiderweb of lines. A

moment later, all blue fades from the surface. The panel before me returns to being a simple mirror once more.

Kir.

I turn the name over in my mind. That's my real name. It's foreign and familiar, all at once.

I turn to Jacoby. "He called me Kir."

"The name suits you." Jacoby stares at me in a way that makes my insides curl.

I brush my fingers down the mirror's surface. "I began with one horrible life template as a stepsister. Now I've found another one as a moonbeam elf." I shudder, thinking of the Vassal Wars. "It's just as awful."

"Fae life is rough," offers Jacoby. "All you can do is fight and live."

I scan Jacoby from head to toe. A fierce look shines in his eyes. Once again, I see him as I did while growing up: Jacoby, the determined knight in his stone suit of mental armor. He's all things glorious and bright.

What am I?

Turning, I inspect my own reflection in the broken mirror. The image that looks back isn't the only thing in pieces now. My whole identity feels torn apart.

Perhaps that's not a bad thing.

Maybe the moment has come to push my broken bits together in a new way.

My thoughts turn to Elle. Jacoby sent her a message

about Nal'Adel. That could be some template-shattering news. Right now, my stepsister may be searching for a new future of her own. The more I think about it, the more my magic hums inside me. Sometimes, I know things without realizing why. Now my supernatural foresight tells me that one thing is certain.

Elle and I will soon alter our lives forever.

24

ELLE

I spend so much time trying to cast spells, I end up falling asleep on the living room couch. By the time I wake up, it's late morning.

Ever notice how when you cry your eyes out the night before, then you wake up the next day with your lashes all crusted together?

Me, neither.

Turns out, it does happen and it's disgusting.

Sitting up, I clear the crud out of my eyes and come to a major decision. If I allow myself to get weighed down by grief, it'll crush me like a bug in no time. I must channel my sorrow into something else.

Not a problem.

I'm casting spells and getting answers. My two big

questions are easy enough, namely Who killed Alec? And how do I take that person down?

First things first. I fire up my phone and send off an email to school, saying that I have the flu and won't be in. I'm sure they've seen the news. No one will give me any grief.

Next I get to casting. I launch spells for everything from summoning Alec's ghost to divining the future. Each time, my fairy dust rises into a cloud for a moment. Then it dissolves into nothing.

Clearly, my magic skills need a tune-up.

I try to summon up some spell casting help. At first, I reach out to Colonel Mallory, Bry and Knox. Sadly, I can't get a spell to connect. They must be very out of touch indeed. I know they'd reach out if they'd gotten the news about Alec.

And yes, I worry about them a little bit. Although with a dragon shifter and the Queen of Hearts along, my friends are well protected. Eventually, my thoughts circle back to Alec.

What can I say? I'm a woman on a mission.

Getting living help isn't working, so I conjure up some spellbooks for advice. Soon I've got a pile of leather volumes and tons of reading to do. In no time, my apartment becomes cluttered with open books, coffee cups and pizza boxes.

Finally, I figure out what's going on. My spells are failing because I'm asking for something that's either too hard—like breaking past Colonel Mallory's magical blockers—or simply too generic. Spells work best when you know exactly what you want. For beginners like me, it helps to pose a question.

I make up a long list of stuff to ask.

What happened to Alec?

Who created my stalkers?

What does the Glass Slipper Ball have to do with my troubles?

I use all of these queries in my spells.

Nothing works.

Yet I'll never give up.

That's when I notice it—An orb of aquamarine power hangs nearby.

I know my spell colors. That's Jacoby's magic. and based on the swirl of yellow in the orb's center, this is a long-distance message, Jacoby's sent them before. If I get near enough to the floating sphere, the spell will kick into action.

I take one step closer.

Two.

Sure enough, the colored orb pops. A two-dimensional version of Jacoby's head appears.

"Hello, Elle. Sorry I've been so out of touch lately."

I roll my eyes. "So you're apologizing for avoiding me since the ball?"

In all honesty, I know Jacoby can't actually hear me and reply. This isn't that type of spell. Still, I've been hanging around my apartment with nothing but pizza boxes for company. Seems I need to chat with someone my age.

"I have news for you," continues Jacoby. "There's an elf here in the Faerie Lands. Her name is Nal'Adel and she's the Mistress of Moonshadow."

"I've heard of her."

I spend a lot of quality time on Magic Web, so I already know the story of Nal'Adel. She's famous for what she lacks, and that's a Mistress of Moonbeams.

Jacoby sighs. "Well, I'm not sure how to tell you this."

"Just say it." Even though Jacoby's not really here, I'm actually enjoying this conversation.

"Nal'Adel thinks you are her missing Mistress of Moonbeams. She's working with Alec's parents and the Cynders in order to create a new Glass Slipper Ball. I'll be the designated prince for the evening. Nal'Adel is convinced that my presence will prove irresistible to you."

I snort-laugh. "Right."

"We both know I'm not your ideal prize, but it seems

that Nal'Adel can't imagine anyone not wanting to wed elf royalty."

"Elves." I roll my eyes. "You guys are so full of yourselves."

"Here is the reason for my message. Whatever you do, stay away from that ball. Personally, I plan to avoid it like the plague."

And that works for me. I already had my Glass Slipper Ball with Alec. There's no way I'd ever want to find someone new. Just the thought makes my eyes sting with tears. *How can Alec be gone?*

"There's more," continues Jacoby. "You must go into hiding. The Faerie Lands aren't safe for you with Nal'Adel around. Sadly, your old haunts on Earth aren't much better. Nal'Adel's agents scented moonbeam magic on you. That's how all of this started." Jacoby pauses.

"I don't have any moonbeam magic," I snap.

Jacoby chuckles. "That was me giving you a chance to say that you don't have any moonbeam magic. And that's absolutely true. Still, Nal'Adel has made up her mind. You know how elves can be. My suggestion is to avoid the fae until this nonsense gets sorted out. At some point, Nal'Adel will figure out who you really are and move on. Until then, stay alert and out of sight. I'll send more messages when I can. "

The image of Jacoby dissolves until it's only the faintest outline of his face. Next it vanishes entirely.

Fresh waves of anger pour through my system. Now I know who employed this mysterious L Cloake. It's also clear who recruited Alec's parents and got my own stepfamily into this nightmare.

Nal'Adel.

No doubt, the Mistress of Moonshadow is doing all this to lure me to this Glass Slipper Ball. Draining spells are tricky things. The ritual needs to take place both on Earth and in Faerie.

My eyes widen. *The construction on the L Center stage.* Alec and I marked it as one of our red flags from the infamous binder. Whatever is happening with that stage, it probably has something to do with the draining ritual. Nal'Adel might even be building a fae door to the Faerie Lands. I wouldn't put it past her.

All of which adds up to one thing.

Without a doubt, Nal'Adel is behind Alec's death. My boyfriend would never allow the Glass Slipper Ball to be used as a lure for my death. That's why Nal'Adel had to get rid of him.

Well, I've got news for that evil elf. I know her name now. I can perfect my spells and summon her to Earth. And once I have her, I'll make her pay.

A small voice in the back of my head says that this

isn't who I really am. Revenge only causes more pain; it doesn't bring anyone back from the dead. As a matter of fact, that voice sounds a lot like Bry. And if my best friend were here, maybe she'd talk me off the ledge on this one.

But Bry is gone, along with Knox, the Colonel and the Queen of Hearts. Perhaps that's all part of Nal'Adel's plan.

My anger boils over into pure berserker-style fury. I focus the energy into getting down to work.

I have a lot of casting to do.

25

AGATHA

*J*acoby and I make the long march out of the Seelie Palace and across the misty landscape. We pause near the same place where we first entered.

The silent walk has given me a chance to think through everything that happened with the Moonbeam Mirror.

Jacoby stops and summons an orb of power. No doubt about it. Jacoby's opening a fae door that leads back to his cottage.

I set my hand on his forearm. "We need to talk."

Jacoby lowers his arms; the magical sphere vanishes. "Certainly. What do you wish to discuss?"

"Jacoby, I'm not the Mistress of Moonbeams. Maybe I'm part of her court, but I'm not her."

"You seem rather convinced of that on very little evidence either."

"Of all people, you should know how it works with elves. They toy with each other all the time."

"It's not as common with the Seelie."

"Still, all elves lie and manipulate."

"You don't." He steps closer. "And I try to keep it to a minimum as well."

With every cell in my body, I want to kiss Jacoby. Yet I know that it's a terrible idea.

"Here's the thing," I begin. "I'm the ugly stepsister. That's my life template. I get exiled at the end of the story and spend the rest of my life in misery."

"You're so wrong."

"And *you're* living in a fantasy. All you want is a powerful partner to help protect your life and herd. That's not me."

Jacoby narrows his eyes. "What's this really about?"

I lift my chin. "All my life, I wondered what my elf side meant. Now I know. When it comes to elves, there is only one fairy tale life template. It's to hurt other people before they get to you. I don't want any part of it."

Jacoby's features turn unreadable. "So what *do* you want?"

"I'm going back to New York. My old home is still

there. No one's touched my room at Cynder Mercantile. I can return there and rebuild my life."

Jacoby shakes his head. "Wyrran never said what your role was in the Moonbeam court. You could be a royal. By going back to New York, you're giving up."

"I'm retaking my life."

Jacoby moves even closer. "You must sense what's between us.

"I don't want a prince, Jacoby. Let me go."

Long seconds tick by before Jacoby replies.

"As you command."

JACOBY

For so long, I've wondered if Agatha is lying to me. After the visit to the Moonbeam Mirror, I finally know she always tells the truth.

All of which is why I know Agatha means what she says when it comes to returning to her old life in New York.

"You don't have much control over your magic yet," I declare. "At least, allow me to cast a fae door for you. That way, you can return home safely."

She tilts her head, considering. "All right. Thank you."

I pull in a fresh orb of power and release it. This time, the sphere creates a freestanding archway. On one side of the enchanted stone arch, there's the misty landscape outside the Seelie Palace. On the other, it's Agatha's old room in Cynder Mercantile.

Agatha steps toward the archway, pauses and turns to me. "I ask you one thing. I saw how you pursued Elle over the years. Please leave me alone."

"Of course. I'll never pursue you as I did Elle."

Agatha shoots me a shaky smile. "Good." With that, she steps through the archway and into her new life. Once she's past the threshold, the stone arch vanishes with her.

Ah, poor Agatha.

She still doesn't know how it works with fae double-speak. Of course, I would never pursue her the way I did Elle.

I'll work far harder.

And it's all because I need to make up for my mistakes.

I got so caught up in my own history of betrayal, I rejected the one person who told me the truth. It doesn't matter if Agatha has any power. I want her honesty, strength and laughter in my life.

And I vow with all that's in me that I'll open a new door for us, soon.

I'm done pushing life and love away.

27

ELLE

al'Adel.
Now, I have a name to I use in the questions I pose within my spells. Total break-through. Excitement zings through my nervous system. I've been casting for hours uncounted. Still, I never felt closer to actually avenging Alec than I do right now.

Tapping in my soul, I summon up a fresh haze of fairy dust. The pink sparkly stuff encircles my hands in a fine mist. Time to ask a new question.

"Where can I find Nal'Adel?"

The fairy dust rises and moves into little tendrils that swirl about. I gasp as I realize the truth.

The dust is forming letters. At first, it's just a jumble of random bits from the alphabet. Still, I can't help but bob on the balls of my feet. Magical writing has never happened before.

Alec, I'm getting closer.

"Come on," I urge. "Where can I find Nal'Adel?"

The letters rearrange into three small words. *The Faerie Lands.*

And the dust vanishes.

Thanks for nothing.

I roll my eyes. *Why am I not surprised?* Fairy dust is just as sly as the fae who wield it. I should know, I'm as tricky as they come. Sure, the dust could rise up and give me something useful like actual directions. But why do that when you can spell out three words and be a snarky little pile of magical bitchitude?

Best to try again.

I summon a fresh batch of fairy dust. Once the pink-n-sparkly stuff hovers above my hands, I pose my next question.

"Is there a way to curse Nal'Adel?"

This would really be ideal. A long-distance curse would enact my revenge without me having to leave the city. To be honest, I don't even like visiting Jersey. Hauling my butt over to the Faerie Lands is definitely something to avoid, if possible.

More letters appear in the air. This time, they spell three new words. *Not for you.*

With that, the fairy dust disappears again.

What a crock.

I nibble my thumbnail and think things through. I'm making progress, but this fairy dust is so sneaky. How can I manipulate it into doing what I want?

An image appears. Miss Morningdew.

My teacher wanted me to leave school in humiliation, yet her efforts backfired. I ended up casting my first major spell and transporting myself home. Maybe fairy dust magic acts the same way, at least for those of us who are beginners.

Perhaps if the dust thinks it will embarrass me somehow, I might just get a straight answer.

This could work, but what to ask? Looking back, it helped to start with an easy question and then work my way up. Before it was, *where I can find Nal'Adel?* So that one's taken.

Another option appears.

Closing my eyes, I focus on the magic within my soul. Power streams down my arms. Opening my eyes, I find a haze of pink fairy dust encircling my hands.

Perfect.

"Who's the person most responsible for my pain?"

The fairy dust rises. Once again, it forms letters. I rock on my heels and wait. Any second now, the dust will spell out the name, Nal'Adel.

Easy peasy.

That's not what happens. Instead of Nal'Adel, the pink haze forms a different name entirely.

Skye.

I blink hard, not believing what I'm seeing. "Seriously?" I ask.

The pink haze instantly forms a new word. *Yes.* With that, the fairy dust vanishes once more.

My blood churns with sorrow and rage. If the magic wanted to humiliate me, then it's a major overachiever. The emotions churning through me right now are far worse than embarrassment.

Closing my eyes, I pull on a fresh round of fairy dust. I'm casting another summoning spell.

One guess who's coming over for a chat.

28

ELLE

*H*ere we go. I'm about to cast the mother of all summoning spells.

At first, I bring up a light haze of fairy dust. Then I ask for more. The cloud turns thicker until it not only encircles me, but it fills my entire bedroom. Next up? I'll speak my incantation. This time, I'm done with questions.

I'm making demands.

"I summon Skye!"

The dust quickly congeals into the form of a genie. A warm sense of satisfaction runs through my veins.

I did it. She's here.

Skye flashes me an innocent smile. "Hello, Elle. Have you reconsidered? Ready to become one of us?"

"You've been lying to me."

"What?"

"I cast a spell and asked who is responsible for my pain. The answer was you."

At this point, I expect Skye to quack like a duck or make a silly face, but she turns deadly serious. I've never seen this side of her before. "Whatever I did, it's because I want to do the right thing by everyone. If Kokkivo were here, he'd vouch for me."

My gaze locks on the glass genie lamp upon my bedside table. I assumed that Skye just picked it up at a store. Kokkivo's work is really popular, after all. Perhaps I was wrong.

And maybe I've been mistaken for a very long time.

"You mentioned Kokkivo before." I fold my arms over my chest. "How long have you been watching me?"

Skye sniffs. "You don't want to know."

"No, *you* don't want to tell me because you can't lie. How long, Skye?"

"Years and years. Our kind is dying out. You've always been half-way into a new life template. All you need to do is cross the finish line."

I nod slowly. "I know what this is about. You targeted me because you think I'm weak. All of this is because I don't have wings."

"So what if I did? Think about the possibilities, Elle.

If you become a genie, you can destroy Nal'Adel. Our kind has that kind of power."

My mind sorts through everything Skye has ever said to me. A memory appears. Crossing the room, I pick up the glass lamp. "The night you gave this to me, you said anyone could be imprisoned like a genie."

"Come on, partner. I was just making conversation." She pulls out her gun and shoots the door. Only instead of a bullet, a little sign comes out the end of the weapon. It reads, *boom.*

Suddenly, I can see what Skye has been doing all along. "This whole unhinged thing is just an act. Now you're shooting the door to distract from the fact that I'm getting closer to what *really* happened to Alec. Tell me, yes or no. Is Alec dead?"

Skye resets her gun into its holster. "I don't have to answer you."

"I think you do. You targeted me for some reason and now you're locked in. If you could fly away right now, I'm certain you would."

Skye glares at me. I take that as all the confirmation I'm going to get.

"Answer me," I demand. "Is Alec dead?"

"No."

My legs feel watery beneath me. Alec is alive. *Yes!*

"I'll be moseying on now." Skye conjures a smoke horse and starts to gallop toward the window.

"Stop!" I cry.

Sure enough, Skye waits.

I lift the small lamp in my hand. "Is Alec imprisoned inside an object?"

Skye raises her hands. The room fills with white smoke. Nervous energy zings through my body. Have I pushed Skye too far?

When the smoke clears, I stand inside the Le Charme board room. There's a date and time on the grandfather clock—this is the very morning when Alec died.

I'm seeing the past. And Skye is making it happen.

Inside this vision, an elf in a fancy gown steps out of the darkness. That's got to be Nal'Adel. After all, she's surrounded in shadow. Plus, a dark harvest moon hangs in the window outside.

Nal'Adel raises her arms; dark ribbons of magic shoot out from her palms and cross the room. Turning, I see the target of her spell.

Alec le Charme.

The man I love stares straight into the bands of shadow, yet he doesn't so much as flinch as the dark magic speeds closer.

The desire to protect Alec becomes overwhelming. On instinct, I rush toward him. Sadly, my movement through the scene only makes the smoke break up. Wherever I go, the Le Charme board room returns to being a generic white cloud.

Skye appears beside me. "Hold on there, sister. You're ruining the spell."

This isn't really Alec, I remind myself. Somehow, I force myself to stand and watch.

Ribbons of shadow encircle Alec. His body becomes wrapped up like a mummy and then pulled toward the gemstone that hangs around Nal'Adel's neck. Both the bands and Alec turn smaller as they close in on the purple stone Nal'Adel wears. With a burst of violet light, both Alec and the dark bands vanish.

Nal'Adel taps her necklace. "Welcome to my prison, Alec."

All around me, this scene of the past returns to being nothing but so many white clouds. Skye waves her arms. Then the pale mist vanishes as well.

I set my hands on my throat, right where Nal'Adel's necklace would lay. "Alec is imprisoned inside a stone."

Skye floats closer. "Don't you want to be a genie *even more* now? With our power, you can free Alec and kill Nal'Adel. It would be simple."

I round on Skye. "Everything with you is hidden truths and outright lies. What makes you think I'd ever trust your advice after this? You let me think Alec was dead!

Skye pulls off her Stetson and sets it against her chest. "I meant what I said. I'm only trying to do what's best. Ask Kokkivo if you doubt me."

"Oh, I have no doubts."

Skye sighs. "Good."

"Because I am absolutely certain that you're trying to do what's best for *you*, not me. And definitely not for Alec." Closing my eyes, I pull up more fairy dust.

Skye gasps. "What are you doing?"

"I'm going to the Faerie lands to find Nal'Adel and get back the love of my life."

"You've got to be kidding. You are no match for Nal'Adel. She tricked the Colonel and the Queen of Hearts. Do you have any idea what that means? By going to the Faerie Lands, you're handing yourself over to her. She will drain you and kill you."

"That's my risk to take."

"You're breaking my heart," says Skye. Little by little, she fades into ever smaller rounds of white smoke. Within seconds, she's gone.

Can't say I'm sorry about that.

Focusing on my power, I pump more fairy dust into the room. Soon the air is thick with sparkly pink stuff.

"Make me a fae door," I whisper.

The fairy dust whips across the room. Once there, it soaks into the far wall. The entire room seems to pulse with power and magic.

And the door starts to form.

Vines crawl up from the floorboards to cover the wall. A stone path stretches out over my rug. Pretty little flowers bud within the display.

A flash of pink light appears in the center of new greenery. When the brightness dies down, there's a new addition to my bedroom: an emerald-colored door now sits in the middle of this garden display.

It swings open on its own.

Yes! I pump my fist in the air. Who says you need actual training to open a fae door? I wanted to do it. I did it. End of story.

A second flash of pink light appears. When it vanishes, there's another green door inside the first. *All right, that's not good.* Then the process repeats until I'm staring at a seemingly endless passageway of open doors.

Huh. Pretty sure this *isn't* how a portal into the Faerie Lands is supposed to work.

Not that it's a shock. My spells are all wonky at best. Plus, I've never cast a door to the Faerie Lands before. This looks legit enough. And I'm still wearing clothing, so that's a bonus.

This is my chance. I'm going after Alec, no matter what.

I step through the first door, which instantly closes behind me. I pull on the handle of the next door in line. It swings open with ease. When I step across the new threshold, the second door closes behind me.

All right, this is annoying but doable. At some point, I'll reach the Faerie Lands. So I open the third door and keep going. With every new door, I focus on the same thought.

Alec, I will set you free.

And in this moment, anything feels possible. After all, I figured out Skye's game. Now I'm heading into the Faerie Lands on my own terms. I may not be an expert spell caster, but I'm also not dissolving into someone else's idea of my identity.

I'm Elle Cynder and I choose to live by a Cinderella life template. Whatever lies ahead, I'll kick it in the ass and call it a bitch, just like I always do.

Boom.

The End

The story of Elle, Alec, Jacoby and Agatha continues in FIRE AND CINDER!

ABOUT FIRE AND CINDER

*M*eet the Magicorum: modern folks who are supernaturally locked into fairy tale life templates. For eighteen-year-old Elle, that role is Cinderella. Meanwhile, Agatha is her evil stepsister. Things go downhill from there…

Cinderella On The Run

Elle—never call her Cinderella—has found the love of her life in Alec Le Charme, the prince of a jewelry dynasty. But when Alec gets spirited away, Elle must ditch her Manhattan home for the perilous Faerie Lands. To save Alec, Elle must also swap her glass slippers for a flying carpet. But will switching templates from Cinderella to Aladdin snap Elle's sanity?

Whatever. Bring on the straight jacket. Elle is one Cinderella who's determined to save her prince, no matter what.

Evil Stepsister or Elf Queen?

Agatha always accepted her role as Elle's evil stepsister. Then her life template changes from nasty sibling to evil elf queen. Agatha has one thought on that score. *Thanks but no thanks.* Agatha refuses the regal life, even though stepping away from her crown means ignoring her lifelong attraction to the elf prince, Jacoby.

Then everything changes. Agatha discovers that Elle's life is at risk... and the only way to save her Cinderella is by teaming up with Jacoby. Trouble is, that's a lot of togetherness. Working with Jacoby could easily end in disaster, not only for Agatha's heart, but also for Elle and Alec's lives.

Fairy Tales of the Magicorum
Modern fairy tales with sass, action, and romance
1. Wolves and Roses
2. Moonlight and Midtown
3. Shifters and Glyphs

4. Slippers and Thieves
5. Bandits and Ball Gowns
6. Fire and Cinder
7. Fairies and Frosting
8. Towers and Tithes

ALSO BY CHRISTINA BAUER

FIRE AND CINDER

BOOK 6, FAIRY TALES OF THE MAGICORUM

The story of Elle, Alec, Jacoby & Agatha continues in FIRE AND CINDER!

FAIRIES AND FROSTING

BOOK 7, FAIRY TALES OF THE MAGICORUM

Elle, Alec and their friends return in FAIRIES AND FROSTING!

ANGELBOUND

Check out ANGELBOUND, the kick-ass paranormal romance! Read on for a sample…

PIXIELAND DIARIES

PIXIELAND DIARIES tells the story of sassy pixie Calla and 'her' elf prince, Dare.

DIMENSION DRIFT

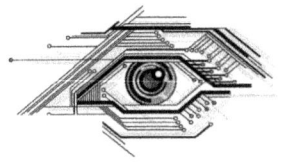

A kick-ass heroine + a swoon-worthy prince + an all-girl heist = SCYTHE!!!

BEHOLDER

Medieval mages … Slow-burn love … And heart-pounding action! Check out the BEHOLDER series!

*I*t's been one month, three days, and six hours since I last 'got my gladiator on' and battled in the Arena. Not that I'm obsessing or anything. Sure, I can sneak in and watch someone else fight, but that's a snore.

I roll over on my dingy bed, scooch under the drab covers, and watch the gray drizzle outside my window. Mondays are the pits.

Mom's voice echoes into my bedroom. "Time to get up! You don't want to be late for school, do you, honey?"

I roll my eyes. *Of course,* I want to be late for school.

Raising my head, I open my mouth to say just that, and then decide against it. Instead, I bite my lower lip, yank the pillow over my head and groan. Loudly.

"Don't make noises at me, young lady." Mom rustles papers in the kitchen. "I've a letter right here. You're on something called the Official Watch List for Unreasonable Tardiness." Her footsteps echo down the hall and pause outside my room. "You'll be suspended from high school at this rate. What do you think about *that*?"

I peep out from under my pillow. Mom looms in my doorway, her fist set on her hip. She's a quasi-demon like me, so she resembles a lovely human with a curvy figure, amber skin, chocolate-brown eyes, and chestnut hair that falls in waves over her shoulders. All quasis have a tail; Mom and I both sport the long and pointed variety. The big differences between us are laugh lines, some grey hair and our opinion of what's 'dangerous' for eighteen-year olds.

I fluff the pillow and slide it under my noggin. Being suspended means no school. Maybe even catching a few Arena matches on the sly. I wag my eyebrows. "And suspension would be bad because?"

"I'd make it that way."

Ugh. She would, too.

Off go my covers. "This is me getting up."

"Good." Mom stomps away.

I shower, pull on some sweats, and sleepwalk into the kitchen, seeing the familiar lime-green appliances,

mismatched furniture, and peeling linoleum tile. Every-
thing looks peaceful, quiet, and empty. Another typical
Monday morning before another average day at school.
BO-ring. I'll have to charm Walker into taking me to the
Arena later. Until I'm called to fight again, it's better
than nothing.

A thick white envelope sits at the center of the
kitchen table. I scoop up and read: "To the Quasi-
Demon, Miss Myla Lewis, 666 Dante Row, Purgatory." I
lick my thumb and run it over the loopy calligraphy.
Real ink. My long black tail flicks in a nervous rhythm.

Frowning, I tap the unopened letter against my palm.
No one sends me fancy stuff like this. In a blur of
motion, my tail darts across my torso, grips the envelope with its arrowhead-shaped end, and tries pulling it
from my fingers.

"Hey now!" My tail's always had a mind of its own.
For some reason, it's decided this letter is dangerous. I
jerk the envelope out of reach, but not before one
corner gets totally shredded. "Now, look what you did."
My tail slinks behind me to curl guiltily about my ankle.

I reread the outside of the letter. Nothing here to
worry about. I *am* a quasi-demon (mostly human with a
little demon DNA). I've spent all eighteen years of my
life in Purgatory (where human souls get judged for

Heaven or Hell, aka the most boring place in the history of ever). This letter's like dozens of others that hit our doorstep each week. Why's my tail on a mission to trash this thing?

I stare at the words again, feeling like they should read: "Open this to turn your life upside-down and your heart into mush."

Clearly, I'm having an off-morning.

I slip the envelope-slash-time-bomb into my mangy backpack. I'll read it later at school.

Mom steps into the kitchen. "How's my sweet baby, Myla-la?" Yes, I'm eighteen years old and Mom still uses pet names from when I was three.

"I'm good." I open a cabinet and pull down a box of Frankenberry cereal.

Mom eyes my every movement, her forehead creasing with worry.

"Did you sleep well last night, Myla?"

Oh, no. Here it comes. I square my shoulders and mentally prepare my 'I'm so very-very caaaaaaalm' voice. "Absolutely." *Nailed it.*

"Any bad dreams?"

"Nope." The 'calm voice' isn't working so well this time.

"Hmm." She taps her cheek. "Met anyone lately? Made any new friends?"

I grit my teeth. All my mornings start off with maternal interrogations like this one. I find it's best to give soothing, one-word answers. "Negative."

"No friends at all?"

"Only the same one since first grade." I raise my spoon for emphasis. "Cissy."

"That's good." She offers me a shaky grin. "You're safe."

I shoot her a hearty thumbs-up. Today's cross-examination ended relatively quickly; maybe Mom's getting less overprotective. A grin tugs at the corner of my mouth.

"More than safe." I speed-chop the air, karate-style. "I'm a lean, mean, Arena-fighting machine." Wincing, I freeze mid-chop. *How could I be so dumb?* Mom loses her freaking mind whenever I say the word 'Arena.'

There's a pause that lasts a million years while Mom stares at me, her face unreadable. Finally, she moves. But, instead of jumping around in hysterics, she flips about and rifles through cabinets in search of a coffee mug.

Wait a second.

This morning Mom cut her interrogation short *and* she didn't panic when I said the word 'Arena.' I wind my lips into an even-wider grin. Sweeeet. Things *could* be changing, after all.

Leaning back in my chair, I watch Mom pour coffee. I know she goes overboard because it's just me, her, and this nasty gray ranch house. I have no brothers, sisters, or straight answers about who my father is, except that he's some kind of diplomat. Add it all up and Mom's a wee bit clingy.

Or, at least, she *used* to be. I drum my fingers on the Formica. A less overprotective Mom opens up all sorts of possibilities. I could watch more matches. I could fight in more matches. I could develop interests in things other than the Arena.

Eh, maybe it's a 'no' on that last thing.

Mom slides into the chair across from mine, her large brown eyes watching me through the wisps of steam curling from her mug. "Want a ride to school today? I don't mind waiting outside the door." A muscle twitches at the corner of her eye. "You know, in case anything happens."

My heart sinks to my toes. Then again, maybe Mom's worse than ever.

"Uhhhh." My mouth falls so far open, some Frankenberry rolls off my tongue and onto the tabletop. Did she *really* offer to stand outside school all day long 'in case anything happens?' Cissy told me how parents get extra-twitchy during senior year. A shiver rattles my spine. My Mom *plus* 'extra-twitchy' *equals* a huge nightmare.

I force a few deep breaths. "Thanks for the offer." It's getting really hard to keep my 'calm voice' handy. "I'll pass this time."

Suddenly, the air crackles with energy. A black hole seven feet high and four feet wide appears in the center of the kitchen.

Out of the void steps a ghoul.

My fingers twiddle in his direction. "Hey, Walker." Technically, he's named WKR-7, but I've called him Walker for as long as I can remember.

"Good morning." Walker nods his skull-like head. If he were a few inches taller, the movement would knock his cranium through ceiling, and he's on the short side for a ghoul. It's a mystery how Walker and the rest of the undeadlies handle an eternity of being so crazy-tall.

Walker pulls back his low-hanging hood, showing pale, almost colorless skin and a strong bone structure. He sports the same hairstyle from the day he died: a brush cut with sideburns and no beard. Great black eyes peep at me from deep sockets.

I grin. It's nice to have Walker around. Most ghouls are obsessed with rules and act irritating as Hell. But Walker? He pushes boundaries like a pro, especially when it comes to sneaking me into the Arena. Having him around is like having a cute and somewhat sneaky older brother, only one without a pulse.

"Be careful, Myla." Walker's thin lips droop into a frown. "That's no way to greet your overlords. I don't mind, but other ghouls could send you to a re-education camp."

I roll my eyes. Purgatory is one massive bureaucracy with the charm of suburbia and the fun of a minimum-security prison. All the work's done by unpaid quasis like me (we're not allowed to call ourselves 'prisoners'). Ghouls keep us in line and make sure we're–*cough, cough*–super happy in our service.

I'm ready to complain about all this to Walker for the millionth time when Mom pipes into the conversation.

"Greetings, my beloved overlord." She's laying it on thick to make up for my sloppy hello. "Want some decaf?" She bows.

Walker nods; ghouls love java.

Mom picks up one of Walker's loopy sleeves, rubbing the fabric between her fingertips. "This is a little thread-bare. Are you here for a new one?" All quasis must perform a service; Mom sews and mends robes. It could be worse. My friend Cissy's mom is a ghoul proctologist.

"No, thank you." Walker eyes the coffee pot greedily.

Mom hands him a full mug marked 'Afterlife's Greatest Ghoul.' Her chocolate eyes nervously scan his face. "What service do you require then?"

Walker frowns. "Myla must battle in the Arena today."

A huge grin spreads across my face. When human souls reach Purgatory, they're given a choice: trial by jury, or trial by combat. Based on the result, they end up either happily floating around Heaven or having their souls consumed in Hell. If the human selects a trial by jury, then it's someone else's problem. But if they choose combat–and the combatant in question is totally evil– then someone like Walker ends up in the kitchen of someone like me. I'm one of a few dozen quasis who kick butt. Literally.

I jump to my feet and clear off my bowl. "Now, this is what I call a Happy Monday."

Mom steps back. "You're sending Myla off to fight today? You can't." She leans against the countertop for support. "Every time she goes, she risks her life." A muscle twitches by her mouth. "Those battles are *to the death*."

I stifle a moan. Mom always focuses on the whole 'to the death' thing like it's the first time she's learned how matches work. Hell, I've battled in the Arena since I was twelve and have yet to get a scratch. You'd think the drama would tone down over the years.

Panting, Mom points to a tattered calendar by the

door. "My little one fought a month ago. She serves once every *three* months, right?"

I raise my hand. "It's not a problem. I'm up for this. Totally."

Mom flashes me a desperate look. "I know that." She grips the countertop like she'll pull it out of the wall. "Please, Walker, tell me it's a mistake."

Walker's black eyes fill with understanding. "Myla must serve today. There's a spike in Arena matches; all fighters have extra battles."

Mom stares at Walker, her jaw grinding out silent rebuttals. After a few moments, she presses her palms to her face, a low sigh escaping her lips. I frown. She's hitting a new level of drama this morning.

Walker shoots me the barest wink. I fight the urge to smile, knowing it means one thing: there's no across-the-boards spike in Arena matches. Purgatory must have an uber-evil soul on their hands, the worst of the absolute worst, and they need their best fighter on it.

That would be me.

Mom shakes her head from side to side. "All those demons and angels. Promise me, you'll keep her away from 'danger.'" She puts special emphasis on the word 'danger.'

"I always do, Camilla."

Mom releases her death-grip from the counter. "Of course."

My back teeth lock. Mom's always going on about protecting me from angels and demons. The demons I understand, but *angels?* Come on.

I zip up my gray hoodie. "Time to trash some evildoers." Stepping to Walker's side, I wait for transport to the Arena.

Mom's hand lightly touches her throat. "Be safe!"

"I'll be super-safe, don't you worry."

"And don't be late for school."

I slap on a smile. "On it, Mom."

Walker bows his head. "Stand back, I'll summon a portal." A new black hole appears in the center of the kitchen. I glance into the darkness, feeling the Frankenberry in my belly come up for a repeat performance. Using a portal feels like tumbling through empty space with a killer case of the stomach flu. Helpful safety tip: hold a ghoul's hand or you'll fall forever.

Taking a deep breath, I grab Walker's chilly fingers so tightly, I'd cut off his blood flow, if he had any. Together, we step into the portal, topple through nothingness, and walk out again onto the sandy earth of the Arena floor.

❧

End of Sample

Order ANGELBOUND, the kick-ass paranormal romance!

APPENDIX

IF YOU ENJOYED THIS BOOK...

...Please consider leaving a review, even if it's just a line or two. Every bit truly helps, especially for those of us who don't *write by the numbers,* if you know what I mean.

Plus I have it on good authority that every time you review an indie author, somewhere an angel gets a mocha latte. For reals.

And angels need their caffeine, too.

COLLECTED WORKS

Fairy Tales of the Magicorum
Modern fairy tales with sass, action, and romance
1. Wolves and Roses
2. Moonlight and Midtown
3. Shifters and Glyphs
4. Slippers and Thieves
5. Bandits and Ball Gowns
6. Fire and Cinder
7. Fairies and Frosting
8. Towers and Tithes
9. Evil Queens and Goblin Kings

Angelbound Origins
About a quasi (part demon and part human) girl who loves kicking butt in Purgatory's Arena

1. Angelbound
2. Scala
3. Acca
4. Thrax
5. The Dark Lands
6. The Brutal Time
7. Armageddon
8. Quasi Redux
9. Clockwork Igni
10. Lady Reaper

Angelbound Offspring
The next generation takes on Heaven, Hell, and everything in between
1. Maxon
2. Portia
3. Zinnia
4. Rhodes
5. Kaps
6. Mack
7. Huntress

Angelbound Lincoln
The Angelbound experience as told by Prince Lincoln
1. Duty Bound

2. Lincoln

3. Trickster

4. Baculum

5. Angelfire

Pixieland Diaries

Sassy pixie Calla loves elf prince Dare. Too bad he hasn't noticed her. Yet.

1. Pixieland Diaries

2. Calla

3. Dare

4. Winter Prince

5. Ley Queen

Dimension Drift

Dystopian adventures with science, snark, and hot aliens

1. Scythe

2. Umbra

3. Alien Minds

4. ECHO Academy

*This is a completed series.

Beholder

Where a medieval farm girl discovers necromancy and true love

1. Cursed
2. Concealed
3. Cherished
4. Crowned
5. Cradled

This is a completed series.

ACKNOWLEDGMENTS

If you're reading my freaking acknowledgements, chances are, I should thank you for something. So, for the record: you are awesome, dear reader.

That said, huge and heartfelt thanks must go out to my husband and son for their rock-solid support. Being an author means a lot of early mornings, late nights, long weekends, and never-ending patience. You two are the best guys in the universe, period.

After that, I must thank the extensive network of reviewers, friends and colleagues who helped me build my writing chops in general. Gracias.

Finally, deep affection goes out to my late, much loved, and dearly missed Aunt Sandy and Uncle Henry. You saw the writer in me, always. Thank you, first and last.

ABOUT CHRISTINA BAUER

Christina Bauer thinks that fantasy books are like bacon: they just make life better. All of which is why she writes romance novels that feature demons, dragons, wizards, witches, elves, elementals, and a bunch of random stuff that she brainstorms while riding the Boston T. Oh, and she includes lots of humor and kick-ass chicks, too. Christina lives in Newton, MA with her husband, son, and semi-insane golden retriever, Ruby.

Stalk Christina on Social Media

Blog:
http://monsterhousebooks.com/blog/
category/christina

Facebook:
https://www.facebook.com/authorBauer/

Instagram:
https://www.instagram.com/christina_cb_bauer/

Twitter:
@CB_Bauer

VLOG:
https://tinyurl.com/Vlogbauer

Web site:
www.bauersbooks.com

COMPLIMENTARY BOOK

Get a FREE novella when you sign up for Christina's
newsletter: https://tinyurl.com/bauersbooks

BEVERLY
HILLS
VAMPIRE

A NOVELLA BY
CHRISTINA BAUER

CLOSING THOUGHTS

*D*ear Readers,

I guess if you're a sports person, you watch an athlete doing energetic stuff and think, *I'd do that differently.*

As you may have guessed, I am not athletically inclined. I do love story telling, though. Whenever I run across a new tale, I always wonder, *how could I make this better?*

Over the years, I've collected quite a list of stuff I want to enhance. Here are two of the big issues I wanted to tackle in BANDITS AND BALL GOWNS…

Moonshadow

I love the song *Moonshadow* by Cat Stevens (now Yusuf Islam). If you haven't heard this song, be sure to check it out. It's such a pretty tune. That said, the words are absolutely terrifying. In case you missed it earlier in the book, check out these sample lyrics:

> *Oh, I'm bein' followed by a moonshadow,*
> *moon shadow, moonshadow...*

This bit is all plinky-plink cuteness, like you're surrounded by a dozen happy kittens frolicking on a grassy lawn. Then that's followed by...

> *And if I ever lose my mouth,*
> *all my teeth, north and south*
> *Yes if I ever lose my mouth,*
> *Oh if I won't have to talk*

Wait, WHAT?

The moonshadow took my mouth?

Damn, that's grim.

Plus, there are a lot more body parts lost in this song. Even so, the *vanishing mouth* always struck me as especially cruel. I concluded that the *Moonshadow* tune should have been expanded so it became a theme song for an elf, considering how it's both gorgeous and deadly.

And I made this decision in high school. Hey, I was still playing Dungeons and Dragons at the time.

Somehow, the way my mind works is that I can pull up stuff like the infamous *Moonshadow decision* decades later. This overall song became the inspiration for the character of Lady Cloake.

Now for the second and larger fix-it project.

Cinderella

I've listed this as one item, but there's actually a ton of stuff that I wanted to enhance in this classic fairy tale. In my book, SLIPPERS AND THIEVES, I sought to answer what I thought were glaringly open issues, like:

- Saying your father is a merchant is super-vague. What did Poppa Cinderella actually do for a living? What was her mother up to all this time?
- I call BS on Cinderella and her prince falling in love on one night. They must have met before. But how?
- I also call BS on the fairy godmother doing

everything for Cinderella, mostly because that
did not happen in the original *Ash Maiden*
story by the Brothers Grimm. I bet Cinderella
had to pull her own butt out of trouble. So
where did she get the guts and plan to make
that happen?

And SLIPPERS AND THIEVES was born. Sadly, I
ran out of pages and time, but I still had more blanks to
fill in. More of this stuff got tackled in BANDITS AND
BALL GOWNS. Examples:

- If you assign spouses to your royal son via
  random dances, then something is super
  wrong in your kingdom. Therefore,
  Cinderella and her prince couldn't have
  ridden off into the sunset. There must have
  been some major shizz to fix after the ball.
  What was it? How did they tackle those
  problems?
- What's the purpose of having two evil
  stepsisters with the exact same personality
  and motivation? *Hello, sloppy storytelling.* Why
  not give one of them some life?
- Once you have a not-so-evil stepsister, she

needs a happy ending and someone to share it with. So who will that person be?

It led to this second book, which I hope you find enjoyable. I certainly had a blast writing it!

Christina